Keep Me In Mind

NAI

U.A.D PRESENTS

URBAN AINT DEAD

P.O Box 448

Maybrook, NY 12543

Cover Design: Talena Tillman / Tdesigns

Edited By: Shawna Brim / Ladies of Lit

Contact Author: FB/IG: Authoress Nai / TikTok: @authoressnai / Email: hoodloverssociety@gmail.com

Contact Publisher at www.urbanaintdead.com

Email: urbanaintdead@gmail.com

Print ISBN: 978-1-969593-08-6

Stay Up to Date

To stay up to date on new releases, plus get information on contests, sneak peeks and more,

Click the link below...
https://mailchi.mp/6d21003686d1/subscribe

Soundtracks

Scan the QR Code below to listen to the Soundtracks/Singles of some of your favorite U.A.D titles:

Don't have Spotify or Apple Music?
No Sweat!
Visit your choice streaming platform and search URBAN AINT DEAD.

Currently on lock serving a bid?
JPay, iHeartRadio, WHATEVER!

We got you covered.
Simply log into your facility's kiosk or tablet, go to music and
search URBAN AINT DEAD.

URBAN AINT DEAD PRESENTS

Like & Follow us on social media:

FB - URBAN AINT DEAD

IG: @uadpresents

Tik Tok - @uadpresents

Submission Guidelines

Submit the first three chapters of your completed manuscript to urbanaintdead@gmail.com, subject line: Your book's title. The manuscript must be in a .doc file and sent as an attachment. The document should be in Times New Roman, double-spaced, and in size 12 font. Also, provide your synopsis and full contact information. If sending multiple submissions, they must each be in a separate email. Have a story but no way to submit it electronically? You can still submit to URBAN AINT DEAD. Send in the first three chapters, written or typed, of your completed manuscript to:

URBAN AINT DEAD
P.O Box 448
Maybrook, NY 12543

DO NOT send original manuscript. Must be a duplicate.
Provide your synopsis and a cover letter containing your full contact information.
Thanks for considering URBAN AINT DEAD.

Introduction

WASSUP, FINE SHIIIIIIII? GET IN HERE & SIT DOWN. ANOTHER SULLIVAN JUST PULLED UP.

CHAPTER 1

Waiting Up For Me

ENZO

I left the house in Park Slope the same way I entered – quiet and untraceable. It was my second hit this week at 50k a body. Both were easy and equally deserving. Hopping into the driver's seat of my car, I checked the time on the dashboard. It read 12:48 a.m. I still had to stop and change clothes before heading to Thyri's place to pick up EJ. It was late by normal standards but right on time for my lifestyle – one that Thyri was slowly starting to understand, although she didn't know what all it entailed.

Today marked a month since I'd hired her as my nanny, and we'd been doing the thing. It was quiet for now, both of us clear on our intentions and considerate of where we were in life. She was adamant about taking things slow and getting to know me. I was cool with that. We'd gone on a few dates, some planned, some last minute with EJ accompanying us. Thyri never seemed to mind him being the third wheel. I thought it was her way of dodging the sexual tension between us.

I was upfront and made it clear that once she gave me the pussy, taking it back wasn't an option. And I meant that shit. I pulled up to my duck off apartment to change, and my phone rang.

"You must've sensed a nigga was thinkin' 'bout you," I said to Thyri as I answered the phone on speaker.

1

"You know I'm telepathic," she replied, giggling. "I was calling to check on you. You know once it gets past midnight, I start to worry."

I smiled. "That or you checking to see when I'm coming to get my rambunctious son."

"Oh, please. You know just as well as EJ that he can pack his bags and move in here if he wanted to at this point."

I thought about EJ attempting to pack his own bags and chuckled. "I'm sure he would. I'm 'bout to head your way in a minute though. You good?"

"Yep," she spoke through a yawn. "I just wanna be up when you get here."

"Aight. You wanna stay on the phone?"

"Ummm, no. I need to hop in the shower. I'll see you when you get here."

I closed my eyes, envisioning her in the shower with soap suds sliding down the crack of her perfect ass.

"Get your mind out the gutter, Enzo."

I snickered. "Damn. I forgot you was telepathic and shit."

"Exactly. See you soon."

"Cool."

She hung up, and I stared at the phone a few seconds before getting out and heading into the building. After changing clothes, cleaning, and breaking down the gun I'd used for the hit, I was back in the car and headed to Thyri's.

As her block came into view, that familiar feeling of peace crept up on me. I'd become accustomed to it whenever I was in Thyri's presence. Parking at the curb behind her truck, I turned my car off and sat there for a few seconds. I always made sure to shake Ezzy after a job. Thyri only knew Enzo, and I intended to keep it that way... for now. Once we decided that we were locked in for the long haul, she'd need to know every part of me.

Stepping out into the cold and onto the sidewalk, I pulled my hoodie over my head. With my phone in hand, I called her once I was at the door.

She answered on the first ring. "You here?"

"Yeah. At the door."

The door opened, and she stood on the other side of it, dressed in silk pajamas with her hair tied in a matching scarf and a wide grin on her face.

"What got you smiling like that this late in the morning?" I asked, leaning against the doorframe.

"What if it's a person and not a thing?" she countered.

My brows narrowed. "Then that person betta be me, or we have us a problem, Mama."

"Good thing I don't want no problems." She pulled me inside by my sweater and closed the door behind me. Still smiling, she pressed her nose against mine. "In case you needed verbal confirmation, the answer is yes." She kissed my lips. "It's you that's been making me smile."

I wrapped my arms around her waist and deepened the kiss. Using my tongue to part her lips, I tongued her ass down at the door.

"Mmmm," she moaned into my mouth before slowly pulling away. "KJ's here."

"Oh, my bad." I pecked her lips once more before stepping back. "EJ still up?"

She blushed and shook her head no. "He's been knocked out for about an hour. He called himself trying to hang with KJ on the game, but he couldn't fight his sleep long enough. Fell asleep with the controller in his hand."

I pictured EJ fighting to stay up, convincing himself that he could do anything a teenager could do. "So, no bedtime routine at your crib but there's one at mine? You out here tryna be his favorite or something?" I joked.

"I'll never try to be who I already am, boo." She winked. "Come on."

I followed her down the hallway, and we stopped at KJ's room. She pushed the cracked door open, and I could see KJ knocked out on the couch he had set up in the room, while EJ lay asleep, sprawled out in his bed. He looked small on the queen-sized bed with a pillow on each side of him.

"KJ set the pillows up, so he wouldn't roll out the bed in his sleep," she whispered.

I nodded my appreciation, noticing that his bed was high up off the ground.

"He wanna be a big dude so bad," I said, shaking my head.

"He does. Let me get him." I watched as she walked quietly into the room and picked him up from the bed. Tiptoeing back to me, she placed him in my arms.

"Hit the light, Ma." I heard KJ say as we turned to leave the room. "Wassup, Enzo?"

"What's good, boy?" I spoke back.

I'd seen a lot of KJ lately since he was always with Cortez. Lil' nigga was cool. Had a presence about him just like his mama.

"His shoes and stuff are in the living room," Thyri said.

We walked back out front, and I laid EJ down on the couch to put his sneakers and coat on.

"I appreciate you waiting up for me. Thank you. And I'm gonna work on not being so late going forward."

She sat on the arm of the couch. "You don't have to thank me. This being something I have to do has turned into something that I look forward to doing. I don't mind waiting up for you, Enzo," she said softly.

"Good to know." I put EJ's hat on and scooped him up gently. He stirred a little, but his eyes stayed closed.

She handed me his bag before walking me back toward the front door, keeping her voice low. "Text me when y'all make it in."

Stopping at the door, I turned to her. "You sound like me."

"I know, huh? I've become just as protective of y'all as you are of me."

"That's a good thing." Opening the door, I stepped out into the night and paused before moving forward. Shifting EJ slightly, I turned back to her again.

"You forgot something?"

"Nah. I've been thinking about something."

Her brow lifted. "Is that a good thing or a bad thing?"

I snickered. "Anything that has to do with me is good. That I can guarantee."

There was that smile again – the smile that did something to a nigga soul.

"Okay. Tell me what you've been thinkin' 'bout then. And make it quick. It's cold, and you got my baby out here a little too long."

"I know you said you wanted to take things slow, and I said I was cool with that, but I just want to put out there what taking things slow mean to me."

"Okay. What's that?"

"Taking things slow for me means forsaking all others. Meaning you only wait up for me." My words were slow for her to get it. Careful to make sure my message was conveyed clearly. And honest for her to know how serious I was.

"Like I said, I don't want no problems. All of that is a yes for me so long as I get the same commitment in return."

I stepped forward and kissed her forehead. "All of that and then some. Good night."

"Good night, Enzo."

I left feeling confident that we'd turned a new page but with the same level of understanding.

Slow didn't mean unsure. Intentional didn't mean timid. For me, I was choosing Thyri without hesitation. And she was choosing to wait up no matter how late I was.

CHAPTER 2

Something To Look Forward To

THYRI

I locked the door behind them and pressed my forehead against it, slowly exhaling. Every interaction I had with Enzo since our first kiss at the Sullivan holiday soirée left me feeling like this – longing for the time to last just a bit longer. It was something about the way he spoke to me. The way his presence filled the room. And his lips. God, his lips really had me questioning whether I really wanted to continue taking it slow. I mean, my mind said it was for the best, but this cat said different.

It had been a little over a year since I had sex. And not because I had sworn off men. And certainly not because I didn't have suitors. A bad bitch with personality that could fill the room always had suitors. However, I was still learning how to be single after coming out of a fourteen-year marriage. I also had a son to think about, and my father's health consumed a lot of my time as well. On top of being selective of who I allowed in my space, I hadn't necessarily put myself out there to date.

And then there was Enzo. He was my type, a provider, protector, an amazing father, loved family, and gave B.D.E. in every sense of the phrase. I was glad that I wasn't closed off to the idea of there being an "us". Still, taking it slow was proving to be more difficult when I was long overdue for coochie maintenance – and not the kind from my wax lady. I was talkin' 'bout fawkin, sweating out my hair type of maintenance.

Shaking off my lust filled thoughts, I went to shut the house down for the night. It was quiet without EJ's voice filling the space. Funny how a two-year-old could take up so much room without trying. I just knew he'd hate it the first time he came over. My place was a nice size, but I didn't have a playroom or amenities fit for a toddler like he was used to having at his fingertips.

It turned out that he loved being in KJ's room more than the one he had at home. He wanted to be a teenager so bad. Smiling to myself, I went into the living room to dismantle the fort me and EJ had built earlier to watch movies in while we ate snacks. We later used it to play hide and seek. Being around him made it hard not to become a big ass kid.

While straightening the pillows on the couch, I thought about Enzo's words.

Forsaking all others. You only wait up for me.

Enzo was dangerous in ways he didn't even try to be. It only pushed me closer to him. Satisfied with my living room, I headed for the kitchen to wash the few dishes in the sink. With my head in the clouds over my new boo, I heard KJ's slippers flapping against the floor as he walked into the kitchen.

"I thought you were sleeping," I said, watching him open the fridge. "Aht aht. You betta wash your hands. I don't know what you be getting into in the middle of the night."

Teenage boys were nasty, and I was almost sure that KJ had long ago discovered himself.

"Come on wit' that, Ma." He huffed but walked over to wash his hands in the second sink.

"I'm just saying. Let's be mindful."

Shaking his head, he grabbed a cup from the cabinet and filled it with water. "EJ coming back over tomorrow?"

"I'm not scheduled to work, but anything can change. Why, wassup? You wanna hang?"

He frowned and side-eyed me over the rim of his cup.

I chuckled. "Why you act like it's a crime to hang out with

me?" I questioned, drying my hands and placing one on my hip. "I think you be forgettin' that ya mama is that girl."

"Ma, no teenager wants to spend time with their moms. Besides, you got someone that wanna hang witchu, but you be frontin'."

I leaned back against the counter with confusion written on my face. "I didn't even know y'all still use that word." I snickered. "Who I'm frontin' on, KJ?"

"Enzo," he replied without hesitation.

My heart jumped, but I remained straight faced. "Huh?" was all I could come up with.

With a wide grin, he set his cup down and leaned back against the fridge. "Ma, I know you've been trying your best to keep the status of y'all relationship from me, but I can see. Y'all tryna act like it's a top-secret mission just makes it even more obvious. I know you're doing it in fear of how it'll make me feel. Enzo doing it out of respect."

"Boy, ain't nobody scared of you." I crossed my arms and playfully rolled my eyes. I knew my son wasn't oblivious, but I also didn't think he was paying that much attention.

He laughed soft and easy, letting me know that he really wasn't trippin' about me dating or who I'd chosen to spend my time with. "You don't have to worry about me when it comes to you dating, Ma. I knew it would happen eventually. As long as dude treats you right, I'm cool. Enzo straight. The family cool too."

I studied my son, who'd been my life for the last fifteen years. He had all of Kaleb's facial features but my heart, no doubt. Here he was, giving me his blessing to live my life for me. I hadn't noticed that his blessing was one of the things that played a part in me taking it slow with Enzo.

"I like him, KJ," I admitted.

"I know, Ma. Do ya thang. I mean, who knows? Maybe he can get you out of that helicopter mama thing you be on." He snickered.

"Boy, please. Me dating or even being in a relationship will never make me back up off of you." I swatted him with the dish towel, and he jumped back.

"Hey, I tried." Picking up his glass, he kissed my cheek. "Just so you know, I draw the line at babysitting."

"Got it. Good night, baby."

"Night, Ma."

He headed back down the hall, leaving me with a smile on my face and my heart full.

He knew, I thought. Relief washed over me, knowing I no longer had to find the right time or the right way to tell him.

I finished shutting the house down, and my phone chimed, indicating a text notification. Picking it up, there was a text from Enzo.

> Enzo: Made it home. He ain't wake up once.

Below the message was a picture of EJ tucked into his bed, still sound asleep.

> Me: He played hard today.

> Enzo: I can tell. Oh, I forgot to let you know we have a date tomorrow night. Just us. Ya boy gotta sit this one out.

> Me: Lol. He won't be happy about it, but it's fine with me. Where we going?

> Enzo: Dinner. We'll see where the night takes us after. And I'll be sure to break the news gently to EJ that he'll be hanging with Grandma for the night. Dress it up and make it real for a nigga too. Heels and all dat.

My mouth formed a sly grin as my eyes cut to my closet.

> Me: I can do that.

I was excited about the date. And while I enjoyed our little outings with EJ, this date would be grown and sexy. He wanted me to dress it up and make it real. I planned to do just that.

I STOOD IN THE MIDDLE OF MY KITCHEN, SLOWLY sipping a cup of hot chocolate, while staring at the Christmas tree I had yet to take down. I'd made a mental note last week that I'd make it happen and had been walking past the tree since then.

"This weekend I'ma get it done," I said out loud in an attempt to convince myself that the task would be completed – just not today. Today was father/daughter day where I dedicated most of my time to hanging out with my father at Sullivan Manor. It was crazy how far he'd come since being at the new facility. Not only was he receiving excellent care daily, but I didn't have to walk around worrying.

My heart was at ease, and I had Enzo's Aunt Fawn and the team she employed at Sullivans Manor to thank for that. Thanks to her, progress was no longer a wish; it was something I was able to track with my own eyes and through daily updates via the facility's online portal. My father had been reaching milestones just by having people around him who cared enough to go above and beyond their call of duty. One of the biggest milestones was his speech. After a few weeks of working with a speech therapist, his speech had cleared up significantly.

Words that he once struggled with now came out clearer. His confidence was back. Then there was physical therapy. He was ahead of schedule and even surprising himself some days with how much he was able to do. And Fawn was there for it all. She wasn't just the owner of the facility. She was the heartbeat who advocated for every patient in the building, the blessing I knew I needed, who gave extra special care to my dad.

Fawn celebrated my dad's wins like they were her own. She checked in constantly, even when she wasn't there physically. Part of me felt like she was filling a void that my dad never knew he had. When he had minor setbacks, she encouraged him, letting him know that she'd never promised recovery would be a cake walk, but it'd be worth it. More than that, she encouraged me. Made sure to remind me that his life wasn't mine and that I could still be the best daughter and show up for him without losing myself.

"Don't let time pass you by because you're trying to be all you can be here," she said. *"Your father will never forgive you if you do."*

I appreciated her words. I also knew they weren't hers alone. My dad talked to her about me. I watched how he watched me every time I came to visit. He saw my tired eyes some days. My dad knew his babygirl. He knew that telling me to do less would only make me go harder.

Now, he had someone else in his corner to look out for him the way I did. It took the weight off my chest, making my days lighter.

"Aight, Ma, I'm leaving." I heard KJ as he walked down the hallway.

"I'm in the kitchen, boo."

"Oh. I thought you were in your room." Walking into the kitchen, he kissed my cheek.

"Where's your hat? It's cold out."

"I'm good," he said, pulling his hoodie over his head.

"It's you having me buy a $400 Louis hat for no damn reason."

"I wore it the other day."

"You need to wear it in your sleep," I joked, making him laugh.

"It's in my bag. I got you."

"Mmhmm." I took another sip of my hot chocolate. "Text me when you make it to school."

"Will do. And remember, I'm going to Cortez's house for the weekend."

"I know," I confirmed. "Call me when you get there."

"Aight."

I watched him start to leave and waited to see if his head was in the right place. He paused at the door and doubled back to grab the garbage. "That's my guy," I said, and he threw up the peace sign as he walked out.

Letting KJ have some of his freedom back wasn't easy, but he worked for it, so I let go of the reins a little. I'd talked to Kaleb about it, and his first question to me was what brought about the sudden change. I was honest, letting him know that KJ had earned it. He still was tight lipped about the exchange that I'd walked in on that made him ban KJ from the projects, but he agreed to allow him some space.

"I'm giving him enough rope to hang himself, but I'm still holding onto this shit tight, Thyri," Kaleb warned.

So far, so good. KJ made sure to check in. He hadn't been in the projects, and everything else was cool. I was satisfied. Finishing my hot chocolate, I headed to my room to get dressed for the day. It was cold out, so the look for the day was warm, cute, and casual.

I threw on a two-piece set, my Chanel lace up boots, an oversized hoodie, and a peacoat. Pulling the scarf off my quick weave, I finger combed through it before pulling a beanie over my head. There was nothing wrong with being cute in the winter so long as warm was in the same category. I tossed my keys and phone into my purse and made my way out of the house.

When I made it to Sullivan Manor, the front desk receptionist greeted me as lively as he did any other day.

"Hey, Thyri. The outfit is tea, honey. Never doing too much but still reminding the gworls of what and who it is." Ty snapped and popped his lips, making me giggle.

I could count on him to have me laughing and to compliment me on what I had on.

"Thank you, boo. How's your morning going?"

"Any morning knowing one of the Sullivan men can walk right through this door is a great morning to me."

I side-eyed him playfully.

"Ooop. I mean any Sullivan but yours, booka. You know I admire them all from afar anyway cause they do not play my type of reindeer games."

While Enzo and I hadn't announced the status of our relationship, the couple times Ty had seen us together was enough for him to make us an item.

"You're a mess. Lemme go see my dad. I'll see you on my way back out."

"Okay. I think they just took him back from therapy. He's doing so good."

"Thank you, Ty."

He blew me a kiss and handed me a visitor tag, which I stuck to my hoodie. I took the elevator up to the second floor where my father was. Entering his room, I found him sitting in his wheelchair by the window. The sun was shining bright on him, and it looked like he was enjoying the view.

"Is that my handsome father?"

Glancing over his shoulder, he cracked a slow smile. "My babygirl."

My face lit up as I crossed the room to get to him. "Hey, Daddy." I leaned down, kissing his cheek. "How you feeling?"

"Strong," he said confidently. "Getting back to my old self slowly."

"That's what I like to hear. How was PT today?"

He shook his head. "They kicked my ass today, Butterfly." He laughed. "But you know I'm built for it. And they ain't gon' do nothing to hurt ya old man. Especially when I have you and Fawn in my corner."

"You betta know it. Speaking of yo' boo, has she been here today?" I took off my coat to get comfortable and pulled a chair over to sit with him.

"Not yet. She called. And who said that she was my boo?"

"Oh, Daddy, please. Y'all act like two people in love whenever y'all around each other. Be smiling so hard I can see y'all back teeth."

He grinned. "You see ya daddy still got it."

"You know I ain't mad atcha, Poppa D." I held out my fist to dap his.

We talked for hours during my visit. Me catching him up on how KJ was doing, my job as the finest nanny that a nigga ever did see, and I even let it slip that I had a date later on with Enzo. Though I had no intention on telling him that, his reaction was cool. It seemed like he already knew the nature of my relationship with Enzo but was waiting on me to bring it up. Still, he didn't pry. And I appreciated it, seeing as Enzo and I were in the beginning stages of dating.

"Thryi."

"Wassup, Daddy?" I looked over at him.

"Thank you," he said, his voice steady and strong. "Thank you for not leaving me."

Tears welled up in my eyes. "You don't have to thank me, Daddy." My voice cracked. "You can always count on me to be here."

"I know," he replied. "I still wanna say thank you. There were days when I wanted to push you away because I felt like a burden." His head dropped, and I got up from my chair and threw my arms around his neck. "I'm gon' get back to the father you know and love."

"You never left," I assured him. Tears blurred my vision as I sniffed. "Just a minor setback. You're still my hero. Still the strongest man I know. I love you so much, Daddy."

"I love you too, Butterfly. My biggest blessing and best gift."

For a moment, I was thirteen years old again, and we were sitting in the living room of our apartment, both lost in our thoughts.

My mother had just left the house, and we both knew she wasn't coming back. The house didn't feel stifled with anger my mother could no longer put words to. I found peace in the moment, and by the way he sat back on the couch, so did he. Only I didn't know how to convey it. So, while I was fine on the inside, my posture must've told a different story because he got up and sat next to me.

"You know I don't know nothing 'bout being a single father,

*but I know everything about being **your** father. We in this together, Thyri. You're my biggest blessing and my greatest gift. I got you."*

That was all the reassurance I needed.

"Oh, I'm sorry. Am I interrupting?"

We both looked up to find Fawn backing out of the room.

"No. You're good," I said, wiping at my eyes.

"You sure? I can come back if y'all need a minute. I should've knocked."

"It's cool, baby," my dad said, winking at me.

I could see Fawn blushing from across the room. "Y'all are too cute. Come on in." I waved her inside.

She had her purse on her arm and an insulated bag in her hand. "I won't stay long now that I see you're here." She kissed my cheek. "I just wanted to make sure he had something to eat. I made that lasagna we talked about yesterday." She set the bag down and leaned over to hug my father.

Watching their exchange, I decided to head out and give them some space. "I'm actually gonna go. I have a few errands to run," I lied. "Y'all eat and hang. Me and KJ will be here on Sunday, Daddy." I put my coat on and grabbed my bag. "I love you. I'll see you later, Fawn."

I left before they could try to convince me to stay. I wasn't about to be the third wheel. Not even for my dad and his boo.

As soon as my butt hit the driver's seat, my phone rang. It was Danae calling. Connecting my phone to Bluetooth, I set it on the car mount to answer.

"He..."

"You busy?" She cut me off.

"For a rude ass ho, I am," I replied, rolling my eyes.

"Seriously, Thyri. Are you busy? I need you." I didn't detect any seriousness in her tone. I did hear a little stress though.

"Nah. I'm not busy. I just left from seeing my daddy. What's wrong?"

"Listen, I desperately need to vent about this lunatic, Aura. Where you wanna meet? And if it's the airport, I got

a bag in my trunk right now if it means temporarily escaping his crazy ass."

I laughed. "One thing you gon' wanna do is vent about that man who you claim you don't want as yo' man. And as your cousin, it's my job to listen. So, yes, I'm free. Not for a flight but something more lowkey like the nail salon."

"Perfect. I need a fill-in and a pedi. I know where we can go too. My treat."

"That's what I like to hear. Send me the address."

"Okay."

I hung up, and the address came through. I could only imagine what Aura had done to my cousin now.

———

I walked into Spoiled Luxury Nail & Spa and spotted Danae at the second station. I'd been to this particular nail salon a few times with her, and the customer service was always top tier. The employees moved fast, but it never took away from the quality of the work. They earned every tip they made.

"Welcome to Spoiled Luxury. Do you have an appointment with us today?" A woman dressed casually in all black with the shop name on her shirt greeted me at the front desk.

"Hey. No appointment today."

"Okay, no worries. What were you looking to have done?"

"A gel mani and pedi. I was actually meeting someone here. That lady right over there." I pointed at Danae.

"Oh, you're Nae's cousin."

I nodded.

"Okay, cool. We have you already set up. Here's your drink menu. You can take a seat at the station right next to her."

"'Preciate it."

She smiled and handed me a laminated card with a list of alcoholic and non-alcoholic beverages, another added luxury. With my menu in hand, I walked over to Nae.

"Hey, boo," I greeted, hugging her from behind.

"Hey, cousin. You smell good."

"Thank ya." Taking off my coat, I draped it over the chair, along with my bag.

"Have you met Marli? She's the owner." She introduced me to the woman doing her nails.

"Hey, love. Nice to meet you," she spoke.

"Nice to meet you too. I love your place. You really did your thing."

She smiled shyly. "Thank you. My baby was a labor of love."

I didn't know why, but when she smiled, my mind went to Enzo. They resembled each other around the eyes and lips.

"So, wassup, girl?" I said to Danae. "How was your day?"

"Peaceful up until you know who called fuckin' wit' me."

Marli snickered and shook her head when Danae spoke.

"Oh, you must know about this."

Nodding, she giggled. "All too well."

"And it ain't a damn thing funny. This man think he run me."

I went to say something when the nail tech assigned to me came over to introduce herself. I picked out my color from the vast collection of gel colors, and she got to work.

"Why don't you just give him a chance, Nae? Ion see no man going that hard behind a woman he don't really want. I can't lie, that nigga luh you." I did my best Glorilla voice, making the ladies laugh.

"Nah. He loves the thought of having something he can't easily access. Aura not slick. He just wanna lock a bitch down, and I ain't ready for that."

"Ooouuu, who flowers?" I heard someone say before turning my head to the entrance, along with everyone else.

There was a delivery guy at the door with a beautiful Eternity Rose arrangement from Venus ET Fleur. I knew that white box anywhere. We all watched as the flowers were handed over to the receptionist who had a wide smile on her face big enough to lock her jaw up.

"Must be nice," Danae sang out loud. "Whoever sent it is very fond of you, my girl," she added.

I nodded, agreeing with her.

"No, honey," the receptionist said as she started our way, "according to the card, someone is very fond of you." She set the box on the table beside Danae with a wink and walked away.

"What? Who the hell would be sending me flowers to the nail salon?"

Marli put her head down as she filed, and I knew who the sender was without her having to open her mouth. I watched quietly as she pulled the card out and opened it with her free hand. She read the card silently then looked back up at Marli.

"Really, Marli? I thought this place was sacred. That's the reason yo' ass kept asking what time I was coming." She swatted at Marli, who had burst out laughing, with the card.

"Girl, I'm sorry. He offered to pay the light bill here for next month. That shit high as hell. I had to do what I had to do. I love you tho." She blew Danae a kiss, jumping back when she swatted at her again.

I laughed. "What the card say?"

She turned to me and sucked her teeth before holding it up to read it. "Next time don't let me ask you where you going, and you don't tell me. Got me footing the bill at Marli place and shit. Your tab is paid for too. Have a good day, Ma."

"Oh, bitch, that's sweet as hell. You trippin'," I said, and my nail tech agreed with an *mmmhmm*.

"That's what I'm saying," Marli added. "My cousin don't be playin' 'bout you, D."

"Cousin?" I questioned. "I knew you looked like Enzo 'bout the eyes and mouth."

"Mmhmm. She one of them sneaky Sullivans," Danae said.

Marli gave her the finger and went back to working on her nails. Danae loved the flowers. I could tell by how she secretly admired them the rest of the time we were in the salon.

After two hours of pampering, massage included, we headed out to our cars.

"What you doing tonight?" Danae asked as she carefully slid her flowers in her front seat, strapping the seatbelt over them.

I got a kick out of her. "Period. Protect them flowers ya man sent you," I teased.

"Shut up and answer my question, chicken head."

"Oh, right. I have a dinner date with Enzo tonight. So, this stop came in handy."

"Awww. Okay. Y'all taking EJ?"

"Not tonight." I pouted. "He said my boy gotta stay with his grandma this time."

"Good. Y'all need more alone time. Enjoy yourself. Let your hair down, boo. I got a date myself."

My brows dipped. "With who?"

"A guy I met at the mall a couple weeks ago. I think I told you about him." Opening her door, she slid into the seat.

"No, you didn't. But send me all the information. Picture included. You are not slick." I got in my car and rolled the window down. "I'm not playing either, Nae."

"I know. I'ma send it." She smirked. "Soon as I get home."

"Yeah. You betta or else I'm telling Aura."

"You wouldn't dare, heffa. I love you. Text when you make it in."

I giggled. "You right. And okay."

She pulled off, and I went to do the same when my phone chimed. Looking down at it, I saw a text from Enzo that instantly made me light up.

> Enzo: Been thinkin' 'bout you all day. Lookin' forward to seeing what you have on later.
> Hope yo' day going smooth.

> Me: My day has been great so far. Lookin' forward to you makin' it even better later.

"Ooouu, bitch, you ballsy, ain't you?" I said to myself, ready to give this date my all... literally.

CHAPTER 3

I Can't Shake Him

DANAE

One thing I hated was to be put on the spot, and Aura had a habit of finding a way of doing that every time. He always had a way of making a statement without saying a word. Hell, he didn't even have to be around to make a statement. Gestures that may have seemed small to him, routine even when it came to me, always hit me harder than the ones before. Because why would this man send flowers to the damn nail salon? I reached over to adjust the seatbelt, making sure they were secure as I drove. They were so pretty.

Another gift. Another way of him reminding me that he was around. Another way of him reminding me of who he was and that he wasn't going nowhere. And through all the gestures, he never looked for a "thank you" which somehow made it even harder to shake his ass.

My feelings for Aura were so complicated. I didn't think words existed for them yet. None that I wanted to express out loud at least. It wasn't that I didn't like him or even love him. However, loving him was dangerous because of who he was and who I used to be.

I pulled into the garage of my building and parked my car in my reserved spot. Glancing over at the flowers, the memory of how we met came to me fast.

I was on second shift at Sullivan's Diner, and it was busy as always. A good busy though. One that kept me moving and endless tips in my pocket. It was a hot summer day, and I'd been waitressing. I was always assigned the larger tables because I was the most efficient of the staff. Having only been working at the diner for six months, I quickly found my footing. I blended in with the staff and kept up the moral. I'd become familiar with the Sullivans that passed through also. Some loud. Very few of them quiet. All powerful in their own way.

And then there was Aura Sullivan. He wasn't the oldest, but he was the HNIC.

He'd come in with a few of his boys, sliding into the booth easy like the space was custom tailored to him. Aura was calm, confident, playful on the outside, but he had an air about him that said he didn't fuck around. It didn't announce itself loudly, but you knew it. I kept my distance, not because of the energy he exuded but because I was sweating so bad in a turtleneck sweater I had no busy wearing in July.

Even with the coolness inside the diner, I was still burning up due to all the moving around I was doing. But I kept my sleeves down and still tended to business with a smile. I was always taught to remain professional, no matter the circumstances. In my case, no matter how much the shirt was smothering me.

As Aura and his party finished up their meal, his sister, Amil, who was also the owner of Sullivan Diner, asked if I could collect their check and bus their table. I found it odd that she was requesting I do it, but I brushed it off and went to do as she asked.

"You guys all done here?" I asked, wanting to be courteous.

"Yeah, shorty," Aura spoke for the table. "You can go head and do your thing."

"We 'bout to go outside and blow it down," one of his people said, sliding out of the booth. "Pardon me, Miss."

The rest of the crew followed, while Aura remained seated. Odd, but I shrugged it off and worked around him. They'd made my job easy by stacking their plates and pushing them to the middle of the table. I was so used to working fast from muscle memory that I slipped and pushed my sleeves up without thinking.

"What happened to your wrist?" he questioned like it was his place to do so.

My body went cold. "What?" I replied, and he reached out, swiping his finger over a fading bruise that I thought I'd hidden well with a little concealer. I snatched my arm back as if he'd burned me.

"Is it the same reason you're rocking that turtleneck in this heat?" He asked another question before I could come up with an excuse for the first.

"I..." My voice got caught in my throat. "I'm anemic."

He cracked a smile and nodded. Standing, he held the signed check up to me, along with a $100 tip. "You know, there ain't nothing that a .380 and good aim can't handle, shorty. You make sure to get that anemia checked out. I know my sister got a good insurance plan for her employees. Use it." Gently pulling my right sleeve down, he walked off.

I watched his back as he left the restaurant. I felt so exposed. Embarrassed. And a couple of other words I couldn't think of in the moment. But one thing I didn't feel was judged.

From then on, whenever Aura came in to the diner, he watched me silently. I noticed and kept a professional distance once I realized that he was seeking me out. I thought my avoidance would push him away, but it only made him more intentional about interacting with me. It never felt weird. In some ways, I appreciated it, but I never let him know. I was dealing with too much at home to let him know that I saw him see me. And he didn't pressure me about it either. He didn't cross lines – just made sure I was good in his own little Aura way.

And then things changed about a year into me working at the diner. My ex had gone to his final resting place after silently wreaking havoc in my life. Suddenly, I felt like I could breathe again. The genuine spark I had about life had finally come back. It just so happened that Aura noticed too, and when he did, he stopped *quietly pursing me. He spoke to me openly, letting everyone know that I was his, and dared anyone to challenge it – even me.*

The car pulling into the spot next to me pulled me back to the present time. I fished for my phone in my purse and took it out to text him.

> Me: Thank you for the flowers. But you really gotta stop tracking me down through your family. They gon' start lookin' at me crazy and think I'm leading you on.

> Mr.DoTheMost: Ain't nobody lookin' at you crazy witcho dramatic ass. The card said about all I'ma say regarding your whereabouts though. I'm busy. I'll hit you back in a few.

I rolled my eyes while typing back.

> Me: This message wasn't an open invitation for that.

His reply came fast.

> Mr.DoTheMost: I'm busy, bae.

I stared at the screen for a second before locking the phone and tossing it back in my bag. Unbuckling my flowers, I picked up the box and stepped out of the car. Aura got on my nerves so bad, but it didn't stop me from accepting all the gifts he sent my way. I deserved them. He knew it, and I knew it too.

***

I PARKED IN THE LOT OF AN ITALIAN RESTAURANT IN lower Manhattan where I agreed to meet my date. I had overslept and was running a few minutes behind our scheduled time. Being late made me anxious. Being anxious made me rush, and I hated rushing. I was seconds away from cancelling when Dwayne sent a my outfit already laid out, I decided what the hell. Sometimes, you had to wait on the main attraction.

I'd never been to this restaurant before, but by how packed the parking lot was, I imagined that it was a popular place. It was Dwayne's pick, a lowkey spot that he'd heard good things about. He'd offered to pick me up, so we could ride together, even commenting that he knew women usually liked to be chauffeured. Unfortunately for him, all I heard from that was, 'I wanna know where you live', and that shit was out of the question. I didn't do pickups on the first few dates. He laughed it off but said he respected my rule.

Stepping out of my car, I adjusted my coat and caught my reflection in the car window beside mine. Tonight's fit was sexy with a little reserve. A pair of black jeans from Zara hugged my hips just right. I wore a fitted blazer over a black lace bralette that gave a quiet sexy without flaunting too much. The cleavage was glistening too thanks to the BSB body oil I'd rubbed into my skin.

My Tom Ford heels added an extra inch to my height and paired well with my Tom Ford clutch. The bag was big enough to fit my phone, debit and credit cards, some cash, and a butterfly knife for safety measures. My hair was on point too. Water wave curls cascaded down my back. The leather coat I had on hit my ankles, making my walk extra dramatic as I proceeded up to the restaurant door. To complete the fit, I threw on a pair of shades to shield my eyes from any hating bitches that may have been lurking nearby. All in all, once I stepped inside, it wouldn't be hard to spot my fine ass in the room.

Inside, the host smiled as I approached the podium he stood behind. "Good evening. Do you have a reservation?"

"Yes. Part of my party is here. Reservation should be under Edison."

He glanced down at his tablet and nodded. "Oh, yes. The seven o'clock. Right this way."

I felt like he was lowkey trying to take a jab at me by

mentioning the time, like I needed a reminder that I was late. I walked behind him and spotted Dwayne before we reached the table. He sat there, scrolling through his phone, not paying attention to his surroundings.

"Sir," the host called for his attention, and his head shot up.

He smiled when he saw me. Dwayne was handsome and dressed well. Like me, he'd worn all black – a polo, black jeans, and a pair of black Pradas on his feet. His hair looked freshly cut, and his jewelry was modest with the exception of the blinged out pinky ring that sparkled under the lights.

Before standing to greet me, I watched as he turned his phone face down.

Red flag, I thought but kept my face neutral, so he didn't know my true feelings.

"Hey, you," he spoke. "You look good as hell."

"Thank you." I returned his smile, pulling my glasses off.

When the host walked away, he leaned in for a hug. I allowed it up until he angled his mouth toward my neck. Pulling back before he could stake claim to something I hadn't offered him, I flashed a look that said he tried it.

His smile faltered a bit before he recovered. "My bad, boo."

"Mmhmm. You good. Now you know," I politely warned, hoping he remembered not to try it again at the end of the date.

He helped me out of my coat and pulled out my chair. Making sure I was pushed in comfortably, he slid my coat on the back of the chair before taking his seat. We ordered drinks and an appetizer to start. Falling into conversation was easy but felt oddly familiar. Almost too familiar. Like he was running down a checklist of what we'd already talked about via text over the last couple weeks.

"So, you've been managing the diner for..."

"A year." I cut him off.

"Right." He nodded. "That's dope. You looking to own yo' own restaurant one day?"

It took so much restraint not to roll my eyes. "No. I

mentioned that to you over text, remember? I love what I do, but I'll be going into business for myself soon."

"Oh, yeah. You did mention that. My bad. AirBnB host, right?"

"Something like that." I sipped my drink, annoyed that his description of my business venture seemed small.

There was an awkward silence that was cut short by the waitress placing our appetizer on the table.

"Enjoy," she said.

We snacked on spinach artichoke dip, and he picked the conversation back up. Every question he'd asked was one that I remembered from our text thread. Every joke he tried to get off, I'd fake laughed about already. Same cadence as if he'd practiced his delivery before arriving. The shit was exhausting, and I was struggling to stay present.

Realizing that my interest had long ago wavered, I finished off my drink and started to excuse myself to go to the ladies' room. Before I could, the host made an announcement to the dining room.

"Excuse me," he announced over the chatter and clinking glass. "If you're the owner of a white Lexus ES with the license plate ending in 2501, your vehicle is being towed."

My head whipped in the direction of the front door, stomach hitting my feet. That was my car. I jumped up and beelined to the exit, leaving behind my purse and phone. Pushing the door open with heavy aggression, a scream got caught in my throat when I saw my car halfway on the flatbed of a tow truck. The name Sullivan Towing was big as day on the side of it. Standing alongside of it was Pryce.

Pryce was Aura's cousin and the meanest Sullivan I'd ever met. At least that was how he always appeared. Stone faced. A man of few words and even fewer smiles. I usually kept my interactions with him limited when he came to the diner to avoid possible confrontation. But tonight, tonight he had me fucked up. I was ready to go toe to toe with him about my car.

"Pryce! What the hell..."

He looked up with a scowl on his face. "Not in the mood."

I wanted to say, "You never in the mood, grouchy ass nigga. What else is new?" But I held back, watching, as he reached in his pocket and pulled out his phone.

"You think I give a damn about you being in the mood, Pryce? Put my car down!"

"Call your man," he said, handing the phone to me. "Last number on the call log."

My jaw clenched and so did my ass cheeks. I was so furious. If looks could kill, Pryce would be outta here. "That ain't my man," I said, snatching the phone from him.

"Danae, I'll roll over this fuckin' car so quick, that nigga won't have no choice but to buy you a new one. Don't make this difficult. Make the call."

I knew he wasn't playing, so I didn't respond. Hitting Aura's number, the phone rang once before he answered.

"You found the car?" he asked casually.

"Every time I think you can't get any worse, you outdo yourself. Why the hell do you have Pryce ass out here towing my car, Aura?!" I snapped.

"You ever asked me if I like Italian food, bae?" His tone was calm, further enraging me.

"What? Aura, now is not the damn time. Why do you play so much? Like forreal. This is too far."

"When have I ever played 'bout you? It's a rhetorical question, so you don't have to answer. Wrap that cheap ass food up and go home or Pryce taking the car, and I'm coming to get you myself. You don't have long to think about it. You know that angry nigga don't have no patience, and he's charging me by the minute."

"You are insane! And this shit is not cool."

"I might be. You wanna not do what I asked and find out?"

The fact that he even knew where I was let me know that he

wasn't above pulling up himself, so I didn't want to test him. I was fully convinced that this man had a tracker in my ass.

"And in case you're wondering, yes, I track you. You'll never know how, just know that you'll always be safe. In that pretty little head of yours, you think you're not mine, but I can assure you you are. Now, go in there and tell the school safety nigga that Dada said it's time to come home now."

I sucked my teeth and glanced over at Pryce, who looked bored and ready to go.

"He don't even work in school safety." I argued on the goofy nigga's behalf who hadn't even come out to check on me. **"He's a DJ. You think you know it all, and you don't."**

Aura laughed. **"That's what that nigga told you? Yeah, you gotta come home, Ma. If you can't spot game from a lame, then I'm not doing my job. Dwayne Edison works school safety Monday through Friday and DJs at retirement homes when they have events. I'm mad you let that nigga gas you. Then again, that shit wasn't going no further than this anyway. Go get your stuff. I'm already at $400 sitting here on the phone with you."**

On top of being pissed, I was now embarrassed. I didn't bother to ask how he knew all this information about Dwayne. I just handed the phone back to Pryce. "Put my goddamn car down," I demanded with my lips tight. "I'm going to get my stuff."

Pryce nodded and put the phone to his ear. **"Yeah. She going back in."**

I stomped back inside and snatched up my bag and coat without saying a word to Dwayne, who was still seated and looking dumb.

He blinked. "You good? Did they take it?" he asked with his eyes scanning the restaurant.

"No. They didn't, and even if they did, it's clear that you wasn't doing shit."

"Look, I don't know what's going on, but you went outside,

and the host came back and gave me this note." He handed me a white piece of paper.

I cut my eye at him before reading it.

> *This city is big, but my reach is bigger. The woman you're out with is spoken for. I'm not usually a warning typa nigga, but I'll oblige this time due to the circumstances. I hope you enj—wait, scratch that. You better not had enjoyed shit wit' my woman. But yeah, it's a wrap on this weak ass date. If it's a problem, there's a shooter outside waiting to test ya gangsta. However you wanna play it, Dwayne.*
>
> *-The Boss, A. Sullivan*

I folded the paper and put it in my purse.

"You coulda put a nigga up on game that you had a crazy dude lurking, Danae."

I frowned and rolled my eyes. "Why, so you could forget about it when we got here? Just like you forgot that you said them corny ass jokes last week?" I was irritated and knew I'd hurt his feelings if I said anything further. "Have you a good night, Dwayne."

I walked out of the restaurant without waiting for his response. The tow truck was gone, and my car was still in the lot. Sighing, I got inside and started it up. I went to pull away when my phone rang. Seeing Aura's name on the dashboard, I hit ignore. Of course, he sent a text.

> Mr.DoTheMost: I ain't sorry, but I don't like it when you upset either. I don't know if you had a chance to eat but let me know when you make it in, so I can have something delivered.

Picking up my phone to text him back, I typed aggressive as hell.

I set my phone in the cupholder and pulled off annoyed and
clear that no one had ever disrupted my life the way Aura Sullivan's ass did. I couldn't shake his ass, and that was my goddamn
problem.

CHAPTER 4

Pressure

AURA

"When she go back inside, put the car down," I told Pryce.

"Doing that as we speak," he said. "Send that seven thirty."

"Seven hunnit and thirty dollars, nigga?"

"Yeah, nigga. A hunnit for every minute. I was out here for seven minutes and thirty seconds. I'm on the scene, I'm charging."

I chuckled. "This nigga really charging family."

"Hell yeah. This wasn't no emergency, nigga," he replied. "Consider it an inconvenience fee cause you know you wasn't taking that girl car no way."

I leaned back on the couch and swiped my hand over my face. "It was a warning."

"Nah. That was you showing yo' hand."

"Never that. Just me reminding her that I'm omnipresent."

"You know you could just tell her that you love her. The same way you tell the rest of us."

I paused for a second. "This is different. Danae ain't ready for all that yet."

"How you know?"

"Trust me. I know. I'm content loving her from a distance for now and applying pressure when it counts."

"Aight, lover boy ass nigga." He scoffed. "If you like it, I won't question it."

"You don't even like people, so I don't expect you to understand." I laughed.

"Could give a fuck about 'em." He snickered. "Send that bread, my boy."

When he hung up, I opened my text thread and sent Danae a message, letting her know I wasn't sorry and to let me know when she was home, so I could have food delivered. Of course, she said she wasn't telling me shit. I laughed, expecting nothing more than that. Exiting the messages, I opened the DoorDash app and proceeded to search for the Japanese place she liked around her way. Don't ask me how I knew her exact order when I got to it. It was my job to know. Adding the order to the cart, I planned to wait until the tracker showed close to her building before submitting it.

As I went through the prompts to double dash her dessert, I could hear my grandmother's slippers before she entered the living room.

"You wear her down yet?" Grandma Lettie asked with a smile that warmed my heart.

"You eavesdropping, G?" I joked.

"In my house? No. I listen with open ears and clear intentions." She sat down across from me in her favorite chair.

I chuckled. She'd been listening intently since I was a child. And nobody dared to call her out on it cause Grandma Lettie had rank and pretty much did what she wanted to do.

My grandmother's home had always been my place of peace. I'd lost my mother to suicide at thirteen, and Grandma had been my saving grace. She was my father's mother. Under her roof, the weight eased. As the matriarch of the Sullivan family, she was the keeper of our secrets, the balance in any chaos, and the rider whenever we needed her. Grandma Lettie's home was a sanctuary.

So, when my days were long and weeks even longer, I found solace in her living room.

She had a way of making me feel like things would be okay no matter what the situation was. Sometimes, there were small decisions to be made like what property made sense to invest in, where to move money, and who to delegate tasks to. Then others were heavier – whose luck had run out and needed to be put down, who to trust and to what extent. Those decisions followed me every day. Grandma's crib was where I sought clarity the most.

"Right," I replied, sitting my phone in my lap.

"I've been listening to you conspire the whole time I was in the kitchen. That's why you came over here today?"

I smiled. "I come here every chance I get just to breathe and hang out witchu, lady. You know that."

She studied me before breaking out in a small grin. "And to think about that girl."

"I think about her every day," I said unashamed.

She nodded. "This I know. I still remember the night you called me about her. I knew then that she had cracked open a part of you that you'd long ago closed off."

I knew it too.

I still held onto the first face to face encounter I had with Danae at the diner. I remembered the turtleneck she wore in the heat, making it obvious that she was hiding something. Then there was the bruise on her wrist. I knew that me pointing it out may have thrown her off, but I didn't believe in holding my tongue for anyone, especially when pointing out something I felt was a problem. I gave her a few words of encouragement before going about my business, but I didn't forget her face. In fact, I got her name from my sister.

That night, I called Grandma Lettie and asked her to send a special prayer up for Danae. I asked her to pray over her situation and that whatever person or thing that had been causing her pain be removed from her life. And then, I asked that she pray that once Danae was free and whole again, she'd save the most sacred parts of herself for me. Grandma didn't question my why; she just said, "Okay, grandson." I knew it was as good as done.

"I'ma marry that woman," I proclaimed.

She stood, pulling her housecoat close. "I believe you, grandson. There's a step before that though."

"Yeah? What's that?"

"Get her to at least go on a date with you. You over here having cars towed and shit like that's romantic. You 'bout as crazy as yo' damn daddy."

I laughed, and she walked over to kiss my cheek. "I'm gonna head to bed. I love you. Lock up when you leave."

"I love you too, G. Good night."

My phone buzzed in my lap as she left the room.

Sullivan Business: Delivered.

Nodding, I got up and grabbed my coat. It was time to get back to work.

⁂

THE 'DELIVERED' MESSAGE WAS ONE I'D BEEN WAITING on since I touched back down in the city from Tulum a couple days ago. A weekend business trip turned into a week of negotiations and an unexpected partnership that was very beneficial to me and The Sullivan Family. Sliding behind the wheel of my Lamborghini Urus, I sped out of my grandmother's development and made my way into the city. As I hit ninety on the highway, I glanced out my window at the bright night sky. New York moved like it belonged to me. In a lot of ways, it did.

I was Aura Sullivan. If the way I showed up didn't tell you anything, my name alone said enough. My family's name carried weight near and far. Respect, loyalty, and money moved throughout generations long before I settled in my father's nut sack. I'd been carrying the torch as the head for the last eight years.

Before me was my father, before him, Grandma Lettie, and before her, her father. This shit was in our blood forreal.

Each line had made the organization more sophisticated than its predecessor. For eight years, I'd been keeping everything together and running smoothly – quiet when it needed to be, loud enough to where we weren't just heard but felt when necessary. We were good people at heart. A family full of business owners, investors, builders, and givers alike. And at the same time, our underworld operation was stitched into our bloodline, one that people whispered about.

I drove into Brooklyn where the Sullivan Distillery was located, a place where tourists often toured and private events were held when we weren't busy making and packaging the finest spirits to be exported all over the country. One would never know what other goods were imported and held in the brick building. I pulled into the lot, and security was posted up at the doors. Glancing up at the roof, I spotted one of my shooters in their designated position.

Parking in my reserved spot, I got out and walked up to the entrance. "What's good?" I spoke to the guys.

"Wassup, Aura?" They both greeted, dapping me up.

"Drop off went well?"

"Yep," King, the head of security for the distillery, spoke. "They dropped at the dock. We cleared everything, and the crew is handling the rest inside."

"Good looking, King."

He opened the door for me, and I entered the building. Inside, warm lighting cast over the entire upstairs. Polished concrete, exposed brick, and glass separated the space where patrons mingled from where the machinery to make the alcohol was operated. Upstairs was open to the public for people to celebrate, drink, and pretend they understood the craftsmanship, all while having no idea of the full operation that lived beneath their feet. Bypassing the tasting floor, I headed straight for the private elevator behind a door labeled 'Security Only'. A scan of my fingerprint got the elevator moving.

Downstairs was a stark contrast to the liveliness from upstairs. The air was cooler. The lights were bright, but there was no music or ambiance. Just people at work.

"What's the word?" I asked my cousin, Kyiris, who stood at the end of a long, stainless-steel table that was stacked with product labeled by section.

There was coke, pills, weed, and my most recent add on, guns.

Key lifted her head from the iPad and nodded. "We're right where we need to be. Inventory matches up with the order. Taylin and Jay are in the back organizing what's there, and then they'll start putting this away."

"Alright, cool." I shrugged my coat off and hung it on the wall. "Lemme see what you got." I kissed her cheek while taking the iPad from her.

"This a lotta shit, Aura. Good thing I'm always on my A game and a stickler for detail. You ain't give no heads up about this."

"Yeah. You know I don't like to speak on anything until plans are fully executed. Besides, you can't stay on your toes if I let you know everything in advance."

"Mmhmm. You just love to do that secret squirrel shit."

I snickered. "That too. Everything looks good." I handed her back the iPad after making sure the counts were exact.

Taylin and Jay emerged from the back, laughing amongst each other. They were my younger cousins. Both were responsible for distribution from the distillery.

"All is well?" I confirmed.

Jay looked up when he heard my voice. "You know it."

"You took quality to another level, cuz," Taylin added, both walking over to dap me up. "You seen the switches on these Glocks?" He picked up a Glock 19 and marveled at it. Like Enzo, he was a gun connoisseur.

"Yeah. They did they shit." I scanned the table, examining product.

Used to my routine when shipments were in, they worked around me. I didn't cross check inventory because I doubted them. I trusted my family and their abilities. Still, true leadership meant presence.

I watched as they worked for two hours. Product was packed away by area of distribution to make for a smooth pickup process. We moved discreetly and under the radar to make sure things got done in an orderly fashion. It was the Sullivan way.

"Aight. We good to go," Jay announced once the table was cleared.

"Yes. I wanna go home and soak in the tub," Kyiris said, placing the iPad in a safe and locking it.

"Oh, today is shower day?" Jay joked.

Kyiris turned around with a smile. "Yeah. And smack a silly nigga day. You can't do one without the other."

I laughed. They always found a way to go at it whenever they were around each other.

"Lemme walk you to your car, Key. Y'all shut it down here."

"Got you." Taylin nodded. "Night, y'all. Love."

"Love y'all too," Key said, walking toward the elevator. I grabbed my coat and followed behind her.

"Love."

We got in the elevator and stood on opposite sides.

"Did you get the email I sent you?" she asked.

"What email?"

She rolled her eyes. "The email for the "Will You Be My Boo?" Valentine's Day party that I'm throwing."

"Nah. I didn't." I opened the elevator door once it stopped.

"You lie so damn bad. Anyway, it's gonna be on Valentine's Day, and you can't say no."

"I swear when it comes to these events, you think you run everybody. Like nobody can say no."

She shrugged and twisted her lips. "Ooookay. Is that your way of RSVP'ing?"

I burst out laughing as we made it outside. "Man, Key, that's not what I said."

She loved to throw a party. If there was a celebration to be had, best believe Kyiris was having it. It was her shit outside of the many roles she played in The Sullivan Family organization.

"Alright. Well, Danae coming. I wonder if she has a Valentine." She opened her car door and leaned against it.

"She do. It's me. You ain't gotta wonder 'bout shit."

Now, it was her turn to laugh. "Oh, okay. Check your email, nigga. All the deets are there." She got in her car and threw up the peace sign out her window as she drove off.

Shaking my head, I got in my car and checked the tracker app to see where Danae was. According to the app, she was parked home. Navigating to the DoorDash app, I submitted her order.

> Me: I ordered your food, Ma. Only nigga dime you get to eat on is mine.

Exiting the text thread, I pulled off and headed home.
Pressure didn't have to be loud. It had to be felt.

CHAPTER 5

Dress It Up & Make It Real Fa Me

THYRI

I was in the middle of pulling the last few pins from my hair when the doorbell rang. Checking the time on my phone, it was thirty minutes before Enzo was set to arrive. He hadn't texted that he'd be here early, so I wasn't sure who the unexpected visitor was. The doorbell rang twice more, signaling the impatience of whoever was on the other side.

"I'm coming!" I snapped, matching the irritation conveyed in their double rang. "Who is it?"

"It's Nae."

"Girl, I was about to cuss you out knocking like that," I said once the door was open. "I thought you were out on your date."

Danae stood on the other side of the door with her face balled up in frustration.

"Ahh, hell. Come in, boo." She walked inside, and I locked the door behind her. "I gave you a spare key for emergencies. And judging by the look on your face, this visit seems like an emergency."

"It's really not. Just one of those nights. And I don't wanna just let myself in now that you and Enzo are together." She took off her coat and tossed it on the couch, along with her bag as we passed the living room.

39

"You act like you gon' walk in here one day and I'ma be bussin' it open on the couch. And Enzo ain't my man... yet."

"Well, hopefully, you will be soon."

"You'll be the first to know, boo."

Back in front of the mirror, I finger combed my curls to get the perfect bounce in them. In the mirror, I watched as Nae plopped down on the bench in front of my bed, sulking.

"You gon' tell me what went wrong or continue to suck all the energy out the room?"

She exhaled hard before speaking. "My car was almost towed in the middle of my date."

I gasped. "Bitch, shut up. How the he..."

"Aura," she cut me off. "Aura is how the hell. That man had his cousin come and try to tow my damn car after tracking me to the restaurant."

My hand flew to my mouth to stifle my laughter. "You lying."

"About what? The fact that his crazy ass tracked me to the restaurant or planned to have my damn car towed? Cause both statements are very true and you doggish as hell for laughing."

"Wait. I'm sorry. I'm sorry. That man do not play."

"That nigga told me to wrap my food up to go, or he was coming to get me. But wait, it gets worse."

I turned, leaning back against the vanity. "Worse? Girl, how?"

"Why this man knew who I was out with? Down to where he worked. Aura is unhinged."

"Unhinged and in love with you." She went silent, and I turned back to the mirror.

"Lemme help you with these curls back here." She went to fluffing my curls, easily falling into the role she'd been playing my entire life – my second set of hands. "You look real cute, by the way. Sorry for the intrusion."

"Thank you, Nae. And you know it's never an intrusion. You need me, I'm here. You look cute too, by the way."

"Yeah. Thanks. Too bad I done wasted a good outfit." She shook her head and stepped back. "Do a spin so I can get the full effect of the look."

I spun around, landing in a pose facing her. "What you think?"

"Bad bitch. Enzo ain't gon' know what to do witchu."

"Period." I knew I was killing shit the moment I put on the black Roberto Cavalli mini dress. The Tom Ford heels I paired it with was chef's kiss. There was something about a black mini that drove men crazy. I intended to do just that once Enzo saw me tonight.

Her expression went from excitement to deep thought in a matter of seconds.

"Lemme ask you something, Nae. And be honest."

"Wassup?"

"I can never get a real answer out of you, but what's stopping you from giving Aura a chance?"

Her lips got tight, but I could tell by the look on her face that she had so much she wanted to express. Then, the doorbell rang, giving her an escape. I glanced at the clock and knew it was Enzo.

"That's your date," she said. "We'll talk more later."

"Nae."

"I promise we will. Right now, you got a man waiting."

Usually, I would press the issue, but I let her make it tonight. I didn't want to keep Enzo waiting.

"Okay. We gon' talk, and you gon' tell me the real, right?"

"Scout's honor," she assured.

I nodded and walked out front. "Who is it?"

"Enzo," he replied.

I opened the door, and there he stood patiently. Wherever we were headed must've called for us to put that shit on because he did just that. Collared Fendi crewneck sweater, dress pants, a pair of Fendi monogrammed sneakers, and a peacoat that settled perfectly on his broad shoulders. His presence changed the air as we locked eyes. For a second, I forgot Danae was in the house until she cleared her throat behind me.

"And that's how you do it. If y'all wasn't a couple before, y'all damn sure look like one tonight."

Enzo smirked. "Wassup, Danae?"

"Heyy. Lemme go head and get out y'all way." She kissed my cheek and squeezed past us with her coat and purse in hand. "Love you, Butterfly," she said out loud and mouthed, 'Suck his dick, girl,' behind Enzo's back.

"Love you too," I replied, smiling to keep from laughing at her motioning like she was giving head. "Get home safe," I added then ushered Enzo inside.

"You look good as fuck," he complimented. His eyes scanned me from head to toe then locked in on my face.

His gaze held admiration mixed with lust – a look that I'd become familiar with. Whether I was in sweatpants and an over-sized shirt or dressed in jeans and a t-shirt, that look said it all.

"Thank you." I kissed his lips twice. "You look good as fuck too." I grinned. "And you smell amazing."

"Yeah. Something my lil' baby got me for Christmas."

I blushed at him referring to me as his lil' baby. "She has good taste. Wherever we're headed must be exclusive and require a dress code."

"Something like that. I really just wanted to see you in some-thing sexy more than anything else."

"Well," I cocked my head to the side and bit my lip, "how did I do?"

"My dick hard, so I'd say you did damn good."

"Oh, my God." I giggled. "You nasty. Let me grab my coat."

"Wait." He grabbed my hand before I could walk off. "I got you something. If you like it, I want you to wear them tonight."

I squinted, wondering what he was referring to. Still holding my hand in his, he reached into his pocket with his free hand and pulled out a Tiffany's box.

I looked down at the box he held out then back up to him. "Enzo..."

"Open it, Ma."

"No," I said quickly, making him chuckle. "I mean, I can't. I mean, not that I can't. I just..."

"Stop stalling, Thyri. Open the box. I insist."

That insisting shit he did was so sexy, a thin line between 'you have no choice' and 'I really want you to' that only he could tread so easily.

Taking the box from him, I opened it and gasped at the diamond studs glistening in the box. "They're beautiful. You didn't have to do this. I would've been happy with flowers or an Edible Arrangement. You know I love fruit." I laughed lightly.

"I'm aware, but you would've expected that. These seem more fitting. So, how 'bout you put them on, and you can be the Edible Arrangement tonight? I happen to like fruit myself." His mouth formed a lazy smirk that made the seat of my thong wet.

I shook my head, blushing. Removing the Chanel studs in my ears, I put the new earrings on.

"You look even more perfect, Ma." He pulled me to him and kissed my forehead. "Get your coat so we can go, sexy."

I almost skipped off to grab my coat and purse. If the remainder of the night was anything like how it was starting out, I could guarantee that I'd be bussin' it open later.

THE RIDE TO WHEREVER WE WERE GOING WAS A smooth one. We talked about our day and how we'd been looking forward to seeing each other tonight. Conversations with Enzo were never dull. He kept me laughing with jokes on everybody from me and EJ down to the people crossing the street. He sometimes left me speechless, openly flirting and telling me what he planned to do to my body once he got the chance. For the sake of getting slutted out in the backseat of his Lamborghini, I just listened and smiled.

"How's your pops?"

"Really good. He said the therapy has been a little more intense lately but nothing he can't handle."

"That's wassup."

"Yeah. If ya aunt keep treating him so good, I'm afraid he may not wanna come home when it's time. You gotta see them two together. My dad tryna put his mack down, and your aunt keeping him company and making sure he's well fed. My daddy light up when he see her."

"It's that Sullivan charm, Ma. It's on us and in us." He grinned.

"Oh, you ain't gotta tell me."

He picked my hand up and kissed the back of it.

"Yeah. A charmer for sure." We both laughed, and I pulled my hand back playfully.

His phone rang, and he held it up for me to see that it was his mother calling. "How much you wanna bet that's your boy?"

I giggled. "Oh, I know it's him. Look at the time."

He laughed and connected the FaceTime call.

"Hey, your little grown man wanna say good night," she said.

"Aight. Put him on."

She flipped the camera, and EJ appeared, tucked in bed with heavy eyelids.

"Hi, Daddy," he murmured.

"Wassup, man? You going to bed?"

"I not tired yet."

"The hell you are." I heard Ms. Debbie say in the background.

"Sounds like Grandma thinks differently, Big Dawg."

EJ shook his head no.

"EJ, look." Enzo turned the screen to me.

"Hey, you," I said, smiling.

"Hi, Tyri. I not sleepy." He didn't give me a chance to try to convince him otherwise. The way he rubbed his eyes let me know he was indeed tired.

"I know. But it's late, and remember, strong boys need rest. You know that?"

"Mmhmm."

"You want me to do the sleepy time song?"

"Mmhmm." He nodded.

I sang the hook and chorus to Kash Doll's *Baby Boy* lowly. It didn't take long before he closed his eyes and drifted off to sleep.

Ms. Debbie picked up the phone and flashed a thumbs up.

"I'm gon' need you to record yourself singing for nights like this, baby," she said. **"I know my strong suits, and that is not one of them."** We shared a laugh. **"Y'all have a good night and be safe."**

I waved at the screen before handing Enzo back his phone.

"Aight, Ma. Love you." He ended the call and set the phone down.

Stopped at a red light, he glanced at me. "Come here."

"What?" I smirked, leaning over toward him.

Pressing his lips against mine, he put his hand on my thigh. The kiss was slow and intentional, like he was trying to say something that he wasn't able to convey verbally. I was the first to pull back when I heard beeping from behind us. "We gotta go."

He glanced up briefly before pushing us forward. "You are something else. A good something."

I let his words hang in the air, while butterflies filled my stomach. If only he knew.

CHAPTER 6

Need I Remind You?

ENZO

The way Thyri interacted with my son left no room for me to think about what he may have been missing out on with Kennedy not being around. Everything was natural between the two of them. Thyri made EJ feel safe. Their bond was more than a nanny who looked out for a child as part of her job. She'd integrated herself in his life in a way that didn't feel pushy. She belonged there. So much so that it made EJ miss her when she wasn't around. If he wasn't talking my head off about some two-year-old shit, he was talking about his Tyri.

I held her hand in mine, sneaking peeks over at her as we drove. Her fingers were relaxed, intertwined with mine, while she stared out the window, oblivious to the shit she was doing to my heart. Singing to EJ may have been a part of the bedtime routine she had with him, but for me it was something entirely different. It was her going the extra mile for a child that wasn't hers. My child.

I parked in a nearby parking garage, and we walked over to Amavi, a Mediterranean restaurant that had been suggested to me by Kyiris. I wanted to take Thyri somewhere that required her to dress up. She got the memo and exceeded my expectations. Thyri was effortlessly sexy on a daily, but she'd gone the extra mile tonight. I appreciated every curve, the switch in her walk, and that glossy shit she had to reapply when we got out the car because I couldn't keep my lips off hers.

The way she walked beside me – unhurried, steady, and comfortable – her confidence was on 100. Grown woman shit at its finest. There was nothing performative about Thyri. She was the shit, and she knew that. A woman that knew she was the shit couldn't help but to walk with that kind of air. That kind of confidence made my dick hard. **Thyri** made my dick hard.

Inside the restaurant, we were led to a corner table, which I'd requested when I made the reservation. I liked to have a full view of the dining room and exits. I pulled out Thyri's chair, not only because it was the gentlemanly thing to do but because I wanted to get another view of that ass as she sat down. She must've been reading my mind too because she made sure to sit down real slow. Pecking her cheek, I took my seat across from her.

Smiling, she glanced around the space. "This is nice. I like the ambiance."

"I did good?"

"You did great. I've never had Mediterranean food. This should be interesting."

I nodded, feeling the same. The candlelight flickering low in the middle of the table gave a romantic touch. This was different for me. I'd admit I hadn't always been that thoughtful in the past. I'd taken women on dates, but the thought was minimal. With Thyri, I wanted to romanticize everything because she deserved it.

"Hi, my name is Jessie. I'll be your waitress for the evening. Can I start you off with something to drink?" The waitress beamed as she spoke.

"I'll take sparkling water and the Casa Blanca Margarita please," Thyri said.

"I'll have water for now."

"Okay. Coming right up."

The waitress bounced off, all happy and shit.

"She happy as hell, ain't she?"

Thyri giggled. "I was thinking the same thing. They either beating them or paying them really well." We both laughed at her assessment. "You wanna share an appetizer?" she asked, scanning the menu.

"These appetizers?" I repeated with a noticeable frown.

"Yes." She laughed. "Fix your face."

I looked up at her and shook my head. "Don't nothing on that part of the menu sound appetizing, Ma. I read it twice."

Still laughing, she shook her head. "That'll be the highlight."

"The highlight is none of this shit sound appetizing to me?"

"No, silly. The highlight is the memory we're creating," she corrected. "Since we'll be trying whatever we order together, if it's nasty, then we'll have something to look back on and laugh about in the future."

"Oh, you planning a future?" I challenged her reasoning to see if she'd double down on it.

"Maybe. It'll be one of our firsts that we share together."

I leaned forward slightly. "I can get wit' your thought process but believe me when I say you're not about to convince me to eat no beef tartare. I don't care how fine you are or how good the future sound, Ma."

Giggling, she snapped her fingers. "Damn. I guess I gotta be a Sullivan to pull that smooth stuff off, huh?"

I smirked. "It's a skill, Ma."

"Okay. How 'bout we just do entrées? Order something different than what I choose though, deal?"

"Why, so you can eat off my plate?"

She rolled her neck. "Like the woman I am, absolutely."

The waitress returned with our drinks and took our orders. I went with the oven-roasted chicken, and Thyri ordered grilled lamb chops.

"How's everything been down at Sullivan & Co.?" she asked.

"Business is good. Just secured two new contracts the other day. Commercial properties that I'm sure we'll lock in long term."

"Okayyy. Go you. I'll cheers to that." She held her glass up, and I cheered with my water.

"'Preciate it."

Dinner arrived quick, securing the waitress' tip in my head. I wasn't the most patient person by nature, so prompt service was always a plus for me.

"Oh, we gon' eat good," Thyri let out, her eyes roaming from my plate to her own.

"You better than me. You know, seeing as you'll be eating your food and some of mine," I teased.

"And the fact that you're gonna let me is scoring you major points and a kiss." She leaned forward with her lips poked out, and I met her halfway for the kiss.

"Lips soft as fuck," I said, licking mine as I pulled back.

She smiled and cut into her lamb chop. We ate in silence for the most part, except for a few sexy ass moans Thyri let slip as she chewed. That shit had me so turned on, I momentarily tuned out the people in the restaurant just so I could concentrate on listening.

And then I heard my name.

"Enzo." The voice cut through the moment I was having with Thyri.

I looked up slowly to find Kennedy walking over in a black leather dress and a full-length mink. This bitch wanted to be somebody so bad it was sick.

"I thought that was you when I walked in," Kennedy continued, ignoring the coldness in my stare. Her eyes then slid to Thyri, who seemed unmoved by her presence. "Hi, I'm Kennedy," she introduced herself. "I'm EJ's mo..."

"Egg donor," I completed her sentence before she could lie. "This is EJ's egg donor, Ma."

"According to you," Kennedy countered.

"I think the last two years of his life is proof of that. I'm really not sure why you're at this table right now. You know where I stand with you."

Her fake ass smile thinned. "I know where you stand, but I came over here to let you know where I stand. I wanna see my son. And I feel that as two grown adults, we should be able to make that happen. Holding me to the past is not helping EJ at all."

I looked across the table at Thyri, quiet and poised in her seat.

She took a slow sip of her drink and returned my stare. Kennedy was trying to get an emotional response out of me, but I had nothing for her.

She went to speak again when some baldheaded, foreign looking ass nigga in a suit walked in our direction. I could tell by the way he walked up that he wanted the people in the restaurant to think he was someone important. He wrapped his arm around Kennedy's waist, pulling her to him protectively.

"Darren," he spoke with his hand extended to me.

Seeing that I hadn't attempted to shake his hand, he continued.

"I'm Kennedy's husband. It's nice to meet you. Now I can finally put a face to the name."

Something dark came over me as I sat up in my chair. "It's never nice to see a nigga like me under circumstances like this. And the last thing your wife should be talking to you about is a nigga she used to get fucked by."

Kennedy's eyes widened, her husband's turned to slits, and I could hear an 'oh, shit' from Thyri's side of the table. Kennedy should've been the last one shocked about my response. Of the people gathered, she knew how lethal I could be.

"Excuse me?" Her husband final spoke up after taking a few seconds to process what I said.

I discreetly grabbed the knife on the table, or I thought it was discreet until I felt Thyri's hand cover mine.

"Excuse me," Thyri spoke up. "We were having a private dinner and would like to continue to do so."

Although her tone was polite, there was no mistaking the 'get the fuck on' in it.

Kennedy's ho ass husband blinked then nodded. "You're right. We apologize for the intrusion. Come on, babe," he said to Kennedy before guiding her away.

I caught Kennedy's eyes as she looked over her shoulder one last time.

Exhaling slowly, I'd already put a plan in my head to see her again and not under the circumstance she nor her husband would like.

Thyri rubbed her thumb across my knuckles softly. "You want me to go beat her ass for you and EJ?"

Turning my head to her, I chuckled. "Nah. I don't want my woman fighting. I got people who live for that kind of activity if it ever comes down to it. I want you to be beautiful and poised at all times."

"Oouuu, yeah. You have a lot more to learn about me, Enzo. I've never been anyone's dainty princess."

I locked our fingers together and picked her hand up to kiss it. "Well, you can be my dainty queen."

"Who will get a bitch right if and when necessary," she assured with a wink.

I chuckled inwardly, noting that Thyri could get on the fuck shit if she wanted to. I liked me a lil' gangsta, but so long as she was with me, she'd never have to worry 'bout fighting no ho.

I put the Kennedy situation to the side temporarily and focused my attention back on Thyri. We continued eating with no further interruption. She didn't ask in depth questions about who Kennedy was or why she hadn't been around to raise her son. She didn't question my reaction to Kennedy's husband either. Thyri didn't seem fazed at all. She picked up the conversation where we'd left off like the interruption never happened. By the time we were done, she was full off both my plate and hers.

"That was good. Thank you for tonight," she said, sliding her hand back into mine as we exited the restaurant and made our way down the block to the parking garage.

"No thanks needed. They did they thing on that chicken."

"Oh, my God. It was so good. Even better that I was able to eat it off your plate. You were far too kind."

I chuckled. "Yeah. I bet."

"Other than the food, you okay?" she asked, while we waited on the car.

"Never better," I said truthfully. "Anything you wanna know?"

She hooked her arm in mine and laid her head on my shoulder. "I figured whatever you wanna tell me, you'll tell me in your own time."

The parking attendant handed over my keys, and I helped Thyri into the passenger seat. I didn't want to ruin the night, so I opted out of telling her the history of me and Kennedy. I would soon though. It would be necessary after tonight.

WE ENDED UP BACK AT THYRI'S HOUSE AFTER LEAVING the restaurant. It felt different with just her and I alone. We didn't have to look out for EJ or over our shoulder for KJ. We settled on the couch in the living room, her nestled up under me.

"I'm so full, I don't even feel like changing my clothes. I just wanna lay here just like this," she said. "You wanna watch something?"

"Whatever you wanna do is cool wit' me, Ma."

Leaning over to grab the remote from the coffee table, she turned the TV on. "You ever seen *Raising Kanen*?"

"Nah. I stopped watching that *Power* shit when they killed Ghost off."

"Yeah. That threw me too, but this one made up for it. It's better than I thought it would be."

"Aight. Turn it on. If it's wack, I'ma tell you."

"You betta off telling 50 cause I didn't make the show or choose the characters." She giggled. "I'm just a fan."

"Yeah, yeah. Come lay back here."

Instead of taking her position back on my chest, she stretched out on the couch with her head in my lap. "You like me close to you? I don't think EJ would appreciate me cuddled up with you in this manner."

Leaning over her, I smirked. "EJ ain't here. And yeah, I like you close to me."

"You gon' kiss me or hover?" she questioned daringly.

Not one to back down, I grabbed her chin gently and kissed

her. Not a quick peck. It wasn't soft either. There was a hunger and a yearning in the kiss. The position we were in was weird, but we made the best of it until she stopped.

"Hold on," she said.

I sat up straight, giving her a chance to get up. When she did, she threw one leg over mine, straddling my lap. "This is better." Her hands found their way to my cheeks and mine palmed her ass as we got lost in kissing again.

I'd never kissed so much in my damn life. Kissing was intimate, reserved for someone you really fucked with. I wasn't going around just swapping spit with anybody. But Thyri, she kissed me like she wanted the moment to last. She caressed the back of my neck and moaned into my mouth. Her kiss held the type of passion that made a nigga wanna nut in her and lay in it after. I was talkin' making future plans and shit.

I felt my dick getting harder, and there was no doubt in my mind that she was giving herself to me tonight. With one hand still caressing her ass, I used the other to grab her by the back of her neck, pulling her head back. She hitched in a breath when I put my lips to the nape of her neck before sliding my tongue across it.

"Mmm," she moaned, "that's my spot."

I took full advantage of her pointing that out and began to lick and suck on her neck. The passion marks that were sure to be left behind would be evidence of me marking my territory.

"Enzo," she whispered, "I don't wanna take it slow anymore."

Trailing my tongue up her neck and back to her mouth, I sucked on her bottom lip. "Tell me what you wanna do, Thyri."

She stared down at me with low, lust filled eyes. "I'd rather show you." Slowly, she made her way down my body and onto her knees.

I watched as she unzipped my slacks and pulled my dick out. It sprang up like it had been waiting to make an appearance. Licking her lips hungrily, she pushed her hair behind her ears.

"Once I suck it, it's mine, Enzo."

I bit my lip and nodded slowly.

"No, you gotta say it. You saying it means we're on the same page."

"Once you suck it, it's y..."

She didn't let me finish the sentence before she swallowed my dick whole. I didn't know whether to be proud or in awe. My dick wasn't little, and this muthafucka was heavy. At a loss for words that wouldn't make me sound corny, I just pumped in and out of her mouth in a rhythm that wouldn't make her uncomfortable. Her mouth was extra wet and warm, two words synonymous with good top.

By the way she held the base of it and sucked on the head, I knew then that Thyri wasn't just sucking dick for my pleasure. She was enjoying it. And one thing about a woman who enjoyed sucking dick, she always made sure to leave a lasting impression.

"You look so good wit' that dick in your mouth. That's right, take it right to the back of that throat. Take ya time, Ma. Fuuckkkk. Mmhmm."

My head fell back just as she popped my dick out of her mouth and licked from the base of it back up to the head. Saliva dripped from her lips before she sucked it back into her mouth, holding it at the back of her throat and humming.

Sliding it back out again, she looked me dead in my face, eyes watery but still confident. "You can cum," she encouraged.

The confident look shifted to a devious smirk, making it clear to me that Thyri wanted the upper hand. She had me fucked up if she thought I was letting that happen. Pushing her back slightly, I gave simple instructions. "Stand up and take that off."

Her smirk had deepened as she stood, taking a step back and doing as I said. I did the same, and we watched each other undress down to nothing. This was intimacy. I usually fucked with my pants at my ankles and my shirt on if I wasn't in a relationship. It was the quickest way to get in and get out with no attachments. I felt something for Thyri. I knew it wasn't love, but it was something. And I was about to get all in her shit like Tyrese did Yvette in *Baby Boy*.

Sitting back on the couch, I stroked my dick and beckoned her forward. "Come sit that pussy on my face, Ma."

She stepped forward, and I hit the couch for her to climb up. "You betta not make me fall," she let out while placing her hands on the back of the couch for balance.

"Sit," I commanded, grabbing both of her cheeks for guidance. "Don't focus on falling. Focus on making this pussy cum when I tell you to." Slapping her ass hard, I sucked her clit into my mouth.

"Ahhhh," she cooed.

I palmed both cheeks, while she rocked back and forth on my tongue.

"Ohhh, yess. Just like that. Mmmm. Just like that, baby."

The wetter she got, the harder I got. Her moans were turning me on so bad, I tried to suck her whole pussy into my mouth. Honing in on her clit, I flicked my tongue across it a few times then sucked on it. The more I repeated the order, the louder she became.

"Enzo! Ooouuu, fuck! You gon' make me cum!"

I smiled inwardly then slid my thumb in her ass to bring her to where I knew she needed to be.

"Ughhh, I'm cummin'!!!" She writhed over me, but it didn't stop my tongue assault as I sucked the juices that poured out of her.

I wanted to wait until her legs stopped shaking before entering her, but my dick couldn't. I carefully pulled her body down, placing my dick at her center. Again, we had that intense stare off as I slowly sat her down on my dick, filling her up. She fit me like a glove.

"Fuckk," I let out in a low, breathless tone.

"Yessss. Slow, baby. Just like that." The longing in her tone, coupled with her licking her juices off my lips, was enough to make a nigga nut prematurely.

"Damn, girl. You should've told me this pussy was gon' be biting like this."

"You... didn't... ask," she said between kisses.

When she started that rocking back and forth, grinding on my shit, I knew I was gon' be fucked up 'bout her. I'd rather a woman fuck back than to hit that slow grind. That shit was dangerous.

"It's so big, Enzo," she breathed heavily into my ear.

"That dick good to that pussy, Thyri? It's good to you, Mama?"

"Sooo good."

"Ride it. Ride that dick like it's good to you."

I didn't know what clicked in her head, but she placed her hands on my chest and got to throwing that pussy on me.

"You fuckin' right." *WHAP!* I slapped her ass hard. "Ride that dick. Get that nut, girl."

The more I talked, the wetter the pussy got.

"Ooouuu, shit. I'ma cum. You gon' cum wit' me, Enzo? You gon' gimme that nut, Daddy? Ughhh, shit, I'm cummin'."

"Arghhh, fuck. Me too." I pulled her up quick, shooting a load all over her pussy lips.

"You gon' make me fall!" she squealed, while I held her up.

"Relax, girl. I got you." I stood and sat her down on the couch.

"Damn. Had I known it was like that, I would've gave you the coochie the night I stayed over at your house the first time." She giggled.

Leaning over with my dick hanging freely, I kissed her lips. "Well, you done fucked up giving it to me now cause you can't have it back."

Her response was just a smile and a nod. That was all the understanding I needed.

***

WE WATCHED AN EPISODE OF *RAISING KANEN,* AND Thyri fell asleep shortly after. Although I wanted to stay and lay up under her on the couch where we settled for the night, I couldn't rest until after I made a quick run. Taking the spare key she'd given me to lock the door, I walked outside into the dead of night. Hopping in my car, I started it and sat for a minute to give the engine time to adjust to the cold. While I waited, I typed Kennedy's address into my GPS system. According to the map, she lived forty minutes from Thyri's place.

Having driven past the house twice over the last two years, I was familiar with the area. I could cut the drive by ten minutes. I always knew where Kennedy was from the moment we went our separate ways after leaving the hospital. I kept tabs on her from afar in the event EJ ever had a freak accident and needed her O blood type for a transfusion. It sounded farfetched, but I liked to stay two steps ahead.

For the last two years, I'd driven past her house the day before EJ's birthday. I wanted to see with my own eyes what a deadbeat mother could possibly have going on that she would completely dismiss the fact that her son had grown a year older. I figured that God wasn't ready for us to see each other face to face just yet because I could never catch up to her. Taking it as a sign, I never drove by again, but I committed the address to memory. Wanting to go into this with a clear head, I drove in silence.

The thing about Kennedy was that she didn't know boundaries. She also didn't know when she was in danger. And me being who I was, I had no problem reminding her.

Pulling onto the quiet street of her quaint Mt. Vernon residence, I parked three homes down from her. Still dressed in my clothes from dinner earlier, I looked the part of the working class that lived on the block – except it was late and I was Black. Conscious of those two facts, I walked with my head up like I was an invited guest. The same energy pushed me to the back of Kennedy's house and up her patio steps. Like most people, the patio door was unlocked, granting me easy access.

Stepping inside, I navigated the darkness until I found the living room. I settled on the arm of an oversized couch, prepared to wait until the homeowners arrived. Taking out my phone, I sent Thyri a text.

I started to send a kissy face emoji but had to draw the line somewhere. New pussy would have a nigga doing some strange ass shit. Scrolling to my game center on my phone, I started a new game of Solitaire to keep my mind occupied while I waited.

An hour passed before I heard keys in the door.

"Damn, Kennedy. You forgot to set the alarm again." I heard Kennedy's weak ass husband's voice.

The fact that he relied on his wife to ensure that the house was secure in the first place was some ho ass shit in my opinion.

"How is it that we both left here together, yet I'm the one who forgot to set the alarm?" Kennedy countered.

Now, I didn't agree with her on shit, but this one thing I had to give to her. As their footsteps got closer, I concluded that it was just the two of them in the house. I reached over and flicked the light on from the lamp that sat on their end table.

"Welcome home," I said lowly.

"Enzo, what the fuck?!" Kennedy jumped back with her hand on her chest, while her husband quickly threw his hands in the air.

This nigga ain't the protector of shit, I thought.

"Look," he started, "I don't..."

I shook my head no. "I let y'all get y'all shit off at the restaurant, remember?"

He shot Kennedy a quick glance, but her eyes stayed on me and the Glock I'd pulled as I stood up from the couch.

"Okay, cool. I'ma make this real short, so I can get out y'all hair. I just wanted you to see how easy it is to reach out and touch you should I ever feel the need to. Now, I'm gonna make this very clear so that there's no confusion on where I stand when it comes to **my** son. You," I pointed to Kennedy, "you're gonna go back to pretending as if he doesn't exist. You had plenty of chances to make shit right, and you didn't. I don't trust you. I don't fuck witchu. And anything I don't trust or fuck wit' won't be around my seed." I took a step forward so that I was merely a foot away from the couple. "Y'all got a kid of y'all own now. Make that shit work and don't let your guilt be the reason that y'all end up a figment of your child's imagination. You would do well to remember my last name, Kennedy. This shit can and will get ugly if you push the issue."

I sidestepped them, her husband pulling her behind like he was willing to take a bullet for her. I proceeded to the door then stopped. Thinking about the way he approached me at the restaurant, I turned and brought the Glock down over his face.

"Enzo!" Kennedy shrieked as he fell into her.

"Just thought I'd remind you."

CHAPTER 7

Holding Back

DANAE

For the first time in the two years I'd been working at Sullivan's, I was running late. Me – Danae Ariel Anderson – late for work. The statement was unheard of. I'd barely slept the night before. And it wasn't for reasons that made sense like still being pissed at Aura for trying to have my car towed or irritated that I'd wasted a good outfit on a nigga who couldn't hold a decent conversation to save his goddamn life. No, my tossing and turning was due to my stomach rumbling half the night.

I was convinced that Aura was trying to get me sick just to keep me in the house. The food he had delivered messed my stomach up so bad that by the third run to the bathroom, I just laid on the cold tile for relief. I knew I'd eaten a bad batch of sushi. And that sucked because I loved the little Japanese spot by my place. So much for being a return customer after the night I had.

When my alarm went off this morning, my body was too sluggish and my head too heavy to get up right away. After laying in the bed an extra thirty minutes, I pushed myself up and into the kitchen for a cup of ginger tea. By the time I got my stomach to stop rumbling and got dressed for the day, I was twenty minutes past the time I was supposed to leave the house. Frustrated to no end, I couldn't even bring myself to call Amil. Opting to text instead, I apologized for my tardiness and let her know I was on my way.

As the manager of Sullivan's Diner, I prided myself on showing up before the employees and leading by example. This was the first time I'd fallen short, and I didn't like the way it made me feel. I knew I had to shake the negativity before I arrived though. I had to remind myself that I set the tone. Rushing out of the house, I hit the elevator button a few times as if it would somehow become considerate of my need to hurry and come faster.

"Girl, slow down. You act like you gon' get fired or somethin'," I said out loud to myself.

Taking in a deep breath, I let it out slowly to calm my nervous system. The elevator doors opened, and I stepped inside, hitting the G button for the garage. I knew I had to trick my nervous system in order to reclaim my day. There were still things I had to do once I made it to the diner, and I needed to be focused to do it. I couldn't function in chaos, especially chaos that I created in my own head.

When the doors slid open, I walked off the elevator with my face in my phone. Hitting the remote start on my car key, I frowned when I didn't hear the car respond to my command. My eyes scanned the row of parked cars, and my heart dropped once I got to my spot. The space was empty. Panic consumed my body. I lived in a nice area, but even I knew there was no place exempt from crime in New York City.

With shaky hands and a scream caught in my throat, I started to call 911. Before I could get to the dial pad, I saw headlights. The car pulled into the garage slowly, the lights illuminating the concrete as it got closer. I squinted, and then the realization hit me fast. It was my damn car.

Anger overrode my logic as I stepped out in front of the car like my body was a human stop sign. It stopped just a few inches away to avoid hitting me. I watched as the driver side window rolled down with deliberate slowness and knew immediately who was behind the wheel.

"Bae," Aura spoke calmly out the window, not knowing I was two seconds away from wringing his neck. "Move out the way. You already late for work."

"Muthafu…"

"Danae," he cut in. "Remember who you're talking to."

My jaw tightened as I stared at him. "Why do you have my car, Aura?"

He cracked a smile like he'd been waiting for me to ask. "You never texted me back last night, so I had Taylin drop me off this morning after I handled business. Your car was due for an oil change, so I went to get it serviced. Why you riding around with your tank almost on E?"

I cocked my head to the side, not believing how casually he spoke, like this was how normal people behaved. "Are you serious? How did you even get a key to my car, Aura?"

"I used my emergency spare that I told you I had when I bought the car. Get in before you're later than what you already are. Then, you go in there, and people gotta deal with a pretty face and a nasty attitude. Don't nobody want that over they grits and eggs."

I huffed and stomped over to the passenger side. "You're ridiculous. I didn't know the gift came with built in security that I didn't ask for," I said, referring to the car he'd surprised me with last year on my birthday.

"You also didn't ask for the gift. But Dada didn't want you ridin' around in that Acura, so I had to get my baby right." He reached for the coffee cup that sat in the cupholder and handed it to me. "Peppermint tea. And you said considerate wrong. I'm not ridiculous. I'm considerate. There's a toasted egg and cheese croissant in that bag in the backseat if you wanna put something on your stomach. I told them to hold the bacon. I know you don't like that pork on your stomach early in the morning."

I didn't respond as he backed out of the garage, not because I was trying to be rude but because he remembered things that I'd told him during brief conversations. Aura paid attention and held onto every word I said. He even remembered things I didn't realize I shared. It bothered me sometimes, but it also made me feel seen. He wasn't my man. He didn't care that I mentioned that to him every chance I got. Still, it didn't stop him from moving as such.

"Dada made you smile today?"

I rolled my eyes and straightened my mouth. "Ain't nobody smiling. Focus on the road."

I reached in the back to grab the plastic bag from the backseat. Opening it, I pulled out the sandwich. It smelled so good. I was glad that he remembered about the bacon. Figuring that I'd emptied everything out of my stomach, I felt it was safe to digest. Taking the foil off, I bit into it.

"Mmm." I savored the buttery croissant.

We stopped at a red light, and he glanced over at me. "How'd you sleep?"

"I didn't sleep much. The food from last night messed my stomach up."

"Awww, baby, you was shitty? Why you ain't call me? I woulda got on them people ass 'bout my baby."

"It's your fault. And no, I wasn't shitty. Had you let me stay on my date last night, I wouldn't have eaten that bad sushi. You tryna poison me, Aura?" I held my half-eaten sandwich out to inspect it for anything unusual.

"Yo' greedy ass would be dead as fuck if that was the case." He chuckled. "The sandwich almost gone."

I covered the rest of the sandwich up and placed it back in the bag. "I'm onto yo' crazy ass."

"Girl, hush. You know I'd never harm a hair on your head. A nigga just wanna love you forreal. You the one making shit hard."

I shook my head and didn't respond verbally, but my heart did that thing it normally did when he put love and my name in the same sentence. I guess because deep down inside, I wanted to do the same. I wanted to accept Aura's love openly but rejecting it seemed like the best thing for the both of us.

His phone rang as we got closer to the diner. I could see the shift. He straightened his posture, and the ease in his demeanor was gone.

"What's the word?" he spoke into the phone.

I stared straight ahead, minding my business. My body was alert though.

His voice dipped low, and his hand gripped the steering wheel tight. **"That's not the instruction I gave. Put Tay on the phone."**

The car went silent as we rolled into the diner's parking lot. Pulling up to the front, I went to get out, and he placed his hand on my thigh, shaking his head. The gesture wasn't aggressive, but it wasn't gentle either.

"Dead that nigga." His tone was cold, the instruction clear to whoever was on the other end of the phone.

Something inside me shut down momentarily, flashing back to the voice I'd heard a year ago. It was a voice that used calm like a weapon, the same voice that freed me from abuse but also kept me guarded – from him. Right then, my stomach turned, a slow churn of uncertainty mixed with anxiety. Pressing my lips together, I took deep breaths to shake off the queasiness.

"You aight?" he asked, ending his call.

"Yeah," I said too fast. Pulling my keys from the bag, I pushed the door open and stepped out. "Thanks for the ride in my car."

I didn't give him a chance to respond before closing the door and jogging up the steps. The lights were on inside, meaning that Amil had beat me to opening this morning. Turning my key, I entered, the bell chiming, signaling my arrival.

Amil walked out from the back. "Hey..."

"One second," I managed to get out while walking briskly to the back where the employee bathroom was located.

Barely getting the door closed, I ran into the stall and hurled. At this point, I was over myself. I stayed hunched over the toilet a few seconds longer, holding onto the wall to keep me steady. Feeling the wave of nausea pass, I stood up straight and leaned back against the wall.

What the hell is going on? I thought while walking to the sink to rinse my mouth and wash my hands. I studied my reflection in the mirror and noted that my face was a little flushed and my eyes glossed over. It was nothing that my normal game face couldn't hide – to anyone that wasn't paying too close attention anyway.

"I hope this man left," I said to myself, knowing that if Aura was still around, he'd point out the difference immediately.

Unzipping my coat, I walked back out front like my body hadn't almost gave out on me a minute ago. To my dismay, Aura had come inside and was fully engaged in a conversation with his sister when I reappeared. He stood in front of her with his back facing me, while she looked up, flashing me a small smile.

"Hey, boo. You feeling alright?" she asked.

"I'm better. Thank you, Mil."

Aura turned when he heard me speak. His eyes narrowed, sweeping from my head to my feet, then locked back in on my face. "You need a sick day," he suggested.

"No, I don't. I just said I was fine."

"You wanna be, but you're not," he countered.

"Aura, you ain't my daddy or my doctor. You also don't make my schedule or pay me. I'm fine." My tone was stern, but by the look on his face, I could tell I wasn't convincing.

He shifted his eyes to Amil. "Tell her she's taking a sick day."

Amil blinked and cocked her head to the side. "Now you know that shit don't work on me. I'm not telling Danae nothing. She's a grown woman who'll let me know if **she** needs a sick day."

"Exactly." I rolled my neck.

"Cause I know my girl ain't gon' be walkin' round here sick and feel like she can't tell me." Amil looked past Aura and over at me. By her squint, it seemed like she was trying to get me to admit that his assessment was, in fact, correct.

"Ask ya girl if her stomach been fucked up since last night," Aura pushed.

"Oh, my God. Not you tellin' my business," I said, wanting to punch him in the back of his damn head. "All I need is some tea to settle me. Once I'm moving around, I'll be fine."

Aura cut in. "And I got all the tea you need at the crib.

Ginger. Peppermint. I even got some stomach ease shit my grandma gave me. Your face all flushed and shit. You need to sit today out, Ma."

I rolled my eyes hard. He was really doing the most.

"You know I'm always team you, Nae. But you do look like you could use some rest."

"Come on," Aura spoke. His voice was softer, almost as if he were lowkey pleading with me. "Come let Dada take care of you for the day."

My heart responded before my head could shut him down again. His voice wasn't commanded or controlling. The concern was clear.

Amil stepped from around the counter and over to me, blocking Aura's view. "Go home for a little bit and if you're feeling better in a few hours, you can come back for the dinner rush, cool?"

"Not cool." I smiled, rolling my eyes playfully. "But I know I'm not 100%, and I don't want that to affect my work, so I'll leave with him."

"My girl. I'll check on you later." She hugged me then turned to Aura. "Don't get on her nerves, Aura."

"Man, bye," he replied and waited for me to walk toward the front door. "You need me to pick you up anything from the store before we head in?" he asked, opening my passenger side door.

"No, thank you. I have what I need at home. I just want my bed."

"Who said you was going home?"

He closed my door and walked around to the driver's side.

"Aura."

"Let a nigga take care of you without having to go to extreme measures to do so, Danae. For once, just sit back and let things happen. I ain't gon' do shit to you that ain't already written in the stars to be done. I got you. Trust me."

Trust him? I already did. Admit that to him, I didn't know how to.

CHAPTER 8

What's Already Written

AURA

I knew something was wrong with my baby the moment she stepped out the car. Although she moved quickly, her steps were measured, and the color was off on her face too. She was trying to hide the fact that she was sick, but the way she moved told me that she was pushing through just to show up. Danae took her position as manager of the diner serious. It was the reason my sister entrusted so much responsibility to her.

Cutting the engine, I watched as she rushed inside and decided then that she wasn't working today. I entered the diner a few seconds behind her.

"Wassup, sis?" I spoke to my sister, who was seated behind the counter on her phone.

"Morning. What you doing around here so early? You came with Nae?" She walked from behind the counter and hugged me.

"Yeah. I dropped her off. Had to handle some maintenance on her car."

She squinted. "She let you take her car to get maintenance done?"

"Nah." I leaned back against the counter. "I went by her crib this morning to check the car and saw that it needed maintenance."

Her brows shot up. "That's a bit intrusive, Aura. Don't you think?"

"Nah. I don't. It was a good thing I did stop by. She's not feeling well."

Amil snickered. "Bruh, I'ma hold your hand when I say this." She grabbed both of my hands and took a deep breath. "Yo' ass is crazy, and it's giving stalker. I know, scratch that, we all know that you have Danae's best interest at heart. Even she knows that. But I think the way you go about it is a bit much."

I laughed, taking my hands back and placing them on her shoulders. "What you see as stalking, I see as protection. If I see a need, I meet it before she knows there's a need to be met."

She sighed. "Aura, you're no..."

"Let me finish. Y'all so used to niggas doing the bare minimum that a man stepping in and doing the most is foreign to y'all. Well, to some women because it shouldn't be foreign to you or any of the other women in our family. Daddy catered to Mommy, and he doted on you so much that you shouldn't accept anything less."

"And what did Daddy's love do for Mommy?" she shot back. "She left us."

"Daddy's love held her together for as long as it could. But you and I both know that you can't outrun your own mind."

Our mother suffered from depression for years. She had spurts of happiness, but most times, she was sad and closed off. Both she and my dad did their best to hide her condition, but I knew. I asked my dad questions and wouldn't let up until he told me something that made sense. When he did, I tried my best to be my best at all times when I was around my mother. I wanted to be the reason she had good days. I learned later that it didn't matter how beautiful her life was on the outside. She was suffering inside, so much so that she just decided one day that she couldn't do life at all anymore.

Amil crossed her arms and shook her head. "I hear all that you're saying, but in this case, you're not just stepping in. You're taking over."

I met her gaze evenly and shrugged. "I'm a boss, Amil. I only know how to take over. But my intentions have always and will always be pure when it comes to Danae. So, encourage me. Don't try to talk me out of loving her in my love language."

"And what language is that?"

"Real nigga."

Danae walked from the back, face flushed, moving like she was trying to hide the fact that she needed to sit the day out. There was no need in pretending though. I took one look at her and knew her workday was over.

She was silent during the drive to my place. Her arm was in the window, while her head rested against it. There was a crease in her forehead like she was in deep thought. I had the music playing lowly to avoid awkward silence.

"You know this is kinda considered kidnapping, right?" She finally spoke.

"Am I taking you from one place to another against your will?"

"Yes," she answered, and I chuckled.

"You gon' tell the police that if we get pulled over?"

"No," she snapped. "Why would I do some shit like that?"

"Shit, you tell me since you're being kidnapped."

She went quiet and remained that way until we pulled into the private garage beneath my building. Parking her car between my Aston Martin and the Lamborghini, I stepped out. Before I could make it over to her side to open the door, she had already beat me to it. I laughed inwardly. This girl was a trip.

"Come on witcho stubborn ass." I put her key in my pocket and pointed in front of me for her to walk ahead.

PH41 sat at the top of the Ritz-Carlton Residences in White Plains. My realtor, who also happened to be a Sullivan – my cousin, Myia – had pulled out all the stops when she found the place for me. Sunlight poured through the floor to ceiling windows as the elevator opened directly into the penthouse. The panoramic views spread throughout the 10,700 square foot home made for perfect nightcaps. Although I barely saw much of the place, I spared no expense when it came to quality and tranquility.

Every corner of my place was custom, from wide-plank floors to the sculptured lighting I opted for instead of chandeliers. Every wall was decorated in some kind of painting or family portrait. Each portrait represented the Sullivan legacy and my love for family. My place wasn't flashy, but you knew luxury when you saw it. Smoke grey and white with subtle hints of burnt orange was the color scheme throughout the house. It paired well with the imported marble and stone finishes.

Danae's walk slowed once she stepped inside. She quietly observed. Her eyes made their way from the living room to the open kitchen and then to me.

"You live here alone?" she questioned, still standing in the foyer.

I kicked my shoes off at the door and walked around her. "I do. For now. Let me take your coat." She handed it to me, and I hung our coats in the hallway closet. "Take your shoes off and come in the kitchen."

Surprisingly, she did as I asked and followed behind me. Pulling out one of the barstools that sat at the island, I gestured for her to sit.

"How many bedrooms is in here?"

"Six," I said, walking into the pantry to grab the assortment of teas. "Six bedrooms, six bathrooms, and two half baths."

"And you telling me you don't have a small family somewhere? You ain't gotta lie to me, Aura."

I chuckled. "The fact that you think I would is wild. As much as y'all nail niggas to the cross for being honest, the last thing you should think is that. To answer your question though, no, I don't have a small family anywhere. I plan to start one, which is why this place is the perfect size." I pushed the tray of assorted teas over to her. "Pick one."

She picked up the ginger lemon tea and handed it to me. "All this house and you're barely here."

"How you know where I'm at, Ma? You keeping tabs on me?"

Her lip curled. "Umm, no. This place barely looks lived in."

Grabbing a cup from the cabinet, I filled the glass kettle with water and set it on the stove to boil. Turning back to face her, I leaned against the counter with my arms crossed. "Well, move in and fuck some shit up then. Hang your wig on the back of the bathroom door. Have your makeup all over the counter. Hang your panties up in the laundry room to dry. Move in and make my house a lived in home."

She tried to hide her smile, but I caught it, the second one today. I loved when Danae smiled. She was pretty as fuck, and when she flashed her thirty-twos, it reminded me of why I went so hard about her.

"Here's your tea." I set the cup in front of her. "You want honey or sugar?"

"I'm gonna drink it like this."

"Okay."

I watched as she handled the cup delicately, blowing the hot liquid before taking a sip.

"Why do you do that?"

"What?"

"Watch me."

"Because I have eyes, Ma." I snickered.

"You know what I mean, Aura."

"No, I don't."

"Yes, you do. You don't just watch me. You show up in ways I didn't ask for. And even when I push you away, you still find a way to fit into my life. You can have any woman you want, yet you..."

"I wait." I finished her sentence.

"What exactly are you waiting for, Aura?"

"For you to get your mind right," I replied without hesitating. "I wait for you to heal from whatever it is that's keeping you from me mentally."

She paused. Her facial expression said she wasn't prepared for my response. "And what do you do while you wait?"

I cracked a smile. "I send you flowers to the nail shop. I get your car serviced without you knowing. I threaten niggas that think they have a chance witchu."

"You try to get my car towed."

"Yeah. Shit like that." I liked when my baby caught on.

"And who do you entertain while you wait on me?"

"I don't entertain, Ma. I do a lil' fuckin' here and there, but that's about it."

She rolled her eyes hard, setting the cup down in front of her. "You mad?"

She frowned. "About?"

"Knowing that yo' nigga out here fuckin'."

She sipped her tea and sat back on the barstool. "Oh, my nigga ain't out here fuckin'. My nigga would know not to even play wit' me like that. So, no, I'm not mad that you out here free dickin'. That ain't got nothing to do wit' me."

"Free dickin'?" I laughed.

"You heard what I said. I guess I don't understand why you always checkin' for me when there's hoes checkin' for you. Like, give Big Mama a break."

I walked around the island, invading her space. "And what you gon' do when I stop checkin' for you?"

She went silent and stared up at me over the rim of her cup.

"Admit it, Danae. You just as fucked up about me as I am about you. The only difference is I choose to love you out loud, while you run from the inevitable. But I'm here, Ma. A nigga ain't going nowhere. I don't show up for you for brownie points. I show up because I want you to know how good this shit can get. A nigga love you, and I ain't even made that pussy my home yet. You wanna know why?"

She continued to stare blankly.

"Ask me why."

"Why?" she questioned just above a whisper.

"Cause I need this," I pointed to her head then to her heart, "and I want that."

"And what you gon' do wit' it that the last nigga couldn't?"

"Keep it."

She froze, mouth clamped around the rim of the cup. I didn't move. I stayed locked in on her so that she knew I meant every word I said.

"I'm ready to take part in that rest you suggested I take off for," she said.

"I'll show you where you can lay down."

I walked her to the guest bedroom where a king-sized bed with clean sheets and an oversized duvet awaited her. I knew I'd be pushing it if I asked if she wanted to change, so I didn't bother.

"Bathroom is to your left. If you need anything, I'll be in my office across the hall."

"Okay, thank you." She took a look around the room before turning halfway to me. "And thank you for showing up."

"Always," I replied, walking to the door and closing it.

Suddenly, the penthouse came alive, not because her physical presence filled the space but because now, a piece of her heart did too. And once Danae stopped running from what she felt, I had a space for her to land.

A few hours had passed, and I let Danae sleep without interruption. I needed to do some research on a potential investment property, so I stayed in my office for a few, going over floor plans and figures that worked for me. Satisfied with my plan of execution, I found myself in the kitchen. I wanted to make something that would stick to her stomach but wouldn't cause discomfort when she finally woke up.

I propped my phone up, while Grandma Lettie walked me through her chicken and rice soup recipe step by step on FaceTime. She sat in the camera with her glasses sitting on the brim of her nose, watching my every move. If you wanted Grandma Lettie's help, everything had to be precise, from the way I shredded the chicken to the way I cut the celery and carrots. Thanks to a quick Instacart, I had everything I needed to make the perfect pot of soup.

"Turn the fire down, grandson. You can't rush the process," she said, watching my hand as it stirred the ingredients in the pot. "Your mind can't be elsewhere while you're cooking either."

"I'm here, Grandma," I assured, adjusting the burner.

I'd just added the chicken, carrots, celery, and bay leaves to the pot.

"What's on your mind?"

"Work."

"Mmhmm. Your sister called me. She said you convinced Danae to leave work today."

I huffed. "I guess she felt like I didn't receive her advice well, so she figured she'd come to you and have you deliver it?"

She smiled. "That's what y'all all do, grandson."

"Yeah, well, whatever she said I did, I did it. And I'd do it again."

"I'm sure. All I'ma say is you wanna make sure you're not overstepping."

I covered the pot and stared in the camera. "Y'all be confusing caring with overstepping. That shit be losing me. I'm not forcing her to do anything."

"You're directing," she corrected. "It's clear there's a difference, but you can't move faster than someone's heart."

"Now you sound like Amil."

"No, I sound like a grandmother who wants the best for her grandson."

"And I'm what's best for her," I countered, frustration settling in my tone.

She studied me for a few seconds. "Have you ever thought about why she keeps a wall up between the two of you?"

"She's guarded. I told you about her situation from what I assumed."

"And just what if Danae isn't ready for the lifestyle of Aura Sullivan? What if she's shying away from the weight that comes from your name? What if she doesn't want the protection because it comes with a different way of living?"

I stilled, letting her words settle. **"Anything I love is protected no matter what life I live."**

"You ain't gotta tell me. I raised you to be that way."

"I'm realistic, Grandma. I know who I am. I know the weight my name carries. I also know that Danae will fit right in. She already does. You've met her. If you felt she didn't, we wouldn't be having this conversation."

"This is true," she agreed.

I turned the stove off and flipped the camera, so she could see the finished product.

"Beautiful," she complimented.

I turned the camera back to me. **"Danae will be a Sullivan. It's already written."**

Grandma Lettie smiled and nodded knowingly. **"Just make sure that when she takes on that name that it feels like a breath of fresh air and not like you just cut off her oxygen."**

"I hear you."

"Alright, baby. I'll talk to you later. I love you."

"I love you too."

I wasn't trying to convince my family that the way I was going about having Danae was right. I didn't need approval. Their RSVP once I sent out the wedding invitations was just fine with me.

CHAPTER 9

Letting My Heart Decide

DANAE

I woke up feeling like I'd slept on a cloud. You couldn't tell me the mattress wasn't specially made for me from the moment my head hit the pillow. And I knew a good mattress because I owned one myself, but I was ready to take this one home with me. Not that I'd have to steal it anyway. If Aura even thought that it was something I wanted, it was as good as ordered. The thought made me smile involuntarily.

Picking up my phone, I climbed out of bed and left the room to find Aura. The smell of something savory and roasted floated in the air as I opened the door. I made my way toward the kitchen, slowing my pace once I heard voices. I heard Aura's first. His tone was calm and controlled, like he was being mindful of what he said. When he identified the voice on the other end by calling out to her, I smiled. It was his Grandma Lettie.

We met in passing a few times at a couple Sullivan gatherings, and the words of wisdom she imparted into me always left me teary-eyed. It was like she knew my life and knew what to say, kinda like my own mother but without the judgment. From the conversation I caught, she'd been walking him through a recipe. Then, the conversation switched to a different subject that made me listen a little harder. They were talking about me.

They spoke about the way Aura courted me as well as my

resistance to it. While I couldn't see his face, his responses made it clear that he wasn't letting up any time soon. And then, his grandmother said something that even made me think about the reason I'd been forcing my heart closed to him.

"And just what if Danae isn't ready for the lifestyle of Aura Sullivan? What if she's shying away from the weight that comes with your name? What if she doesn't want the protection because it comes with a different way of living?"

I walked back to the guest room as quietly as I could, taking her thoughts with me. Hearing her speak, those words made me realize that I felt the complete opposite. I didn't mind that Aura had a name. And I already had his protection without having a title. I was rooted in who I was as a woman. Being a part of the Sullivan clan wouldn't make me feel less than.

Being Aura's woman didn't scare me as far as what I had to take on. His way of protecting could be a bit much. But what I feared was what his reaction would be once he knew who I used to be tied to. What would he say if he knew that the woman he openly claimed as his knew that he'd taken a life and never spoke anything of it?

I'd been asleep for what seemed like all of five minutes before Byron walked through the door, high and on bullshit. It was one in the morning, and I'd just laid down after putting my apartment back together. It was in complete disarray after one of our many physical altercations that resulted in a busted lip and a bruised back for me. For him, a deep gash on his arm. I felt every part of the fight, while he merely shook it off. One would think that it would make him leave me alone, but this bastard was crazy. Drugs would do that to you.

Before I could brace myself for round three, he pulled me out the bed by my legs. My back hit the bedpost on my way to the floor.

"Ouch!" I shrieked as the pain vibrated up my spine.

"Get the fuck up," he said while pacing the floor like a mad man.

Byron was as dark as night, so while I couldn't fully see his face, the streetlights that peeked through the blinds showed his silhouette as he paced.

My body moved before my mouth could argue. Although I was slow, I knew I had to get up. I knew that if I resisted, it would only prolong the fight, and by the way he was pacing, this nigga wanted to spar. My body ached, but there was no way I was going to just let him beat my ass and not defend myself. So, with all the strength I had left, I stood, took a deep breath, and squared up.

I didn't have much fight left in me, and quite frankly, I was tired of boxing with this man. Tonight, one of us was going to end up in the back of a police car or the back of an ambulance. The blade that sat under my tongue said that I'd be the one posing for the mugshot. In an effort to intimidate me, Byron stared menacingly in the darkness. Having been in this same position with him recently, I knew he was thinking about which part of my body to attack first.

Byron and I were the same height and probably the same weight since he started putting that shit up his nose. But he was still a man, a man who had two times my strength when he was off the drugs. I braced myself as he stepped forward, and then his phone rang. It was a business call. I knew the ringtone because I had assigned it at his direction. Byron was one of those men that acted handicapped when it came to technology.

I felt temporary relief when he stepped back and answered the call.

"Yo." His voice came out gruff and dry, instantly becoming Banga, the man the streets knew. **"Aight. I'm on my way."** He ended the call and walked toward the door. Before leaving, he turned back to me. "I'ma call you. Answer the phone."

"Mmhmm," I replied.

"You heard me?"

"I heard you."

"I love you."

I didn't respond. He knew he'd have to beat those words out of me before I said it back. He hadn't heard them in months. I was sure it hurt his heart more than I hurt his ego, which was why he never forced me to repeat it.

"I ain't playin', Danae. Pick that shit up," he repeated before leaving.

Like clockwork, the call came in ten minutes later. Being on the phone while Byron was out taking care of business used to be cool. In my head, my man was so sprung off me that he had to hear my voice, even when he wasn't around me. As time went on, my silly ass learned that it was his weird way of keeping tabs on me and controlling my day. I didn't realize it then, but I was creating a codependent monster.

"Danae," his voice came through low and somewhat gentle. **"I'm sorry about earlier, baby. I ain't mean to hit you that hard. You know I get caught up sometimes."**

I didn't speak because I was having a hard time digesting the bullshit that had just come out of his mouth. Byron never took accountability. Everything was somehow my fault. God forbid a bitch merely breathed on a Thursday. Unable to trust my voice, I remained quiet.

I could hear gravel crunching beneath the tires, followed by the car door opening. Figuring he'd reached his destination, my finger hovered over the end button.

"Mute your phone," he instructed.

Rolling my eyes, I muted and put the call on speakerphone. I didn't want to hold the line, but I knew he'd likely call out to me at random to make sure I was still present.

"What's good, Tay?" His voice switched again, this time sharper and alert.

My brow went up. Byron never said names while I was on the phone. I heard shuffling and then what sounded like something brushing up against the phone. Assuming he'd slipped it into his pocket, I went back to half listening. I'd taken a Tylenol PM to help alleviate some of the pain in my back once he left, so I was waiting for it to kick in.

"Y'all niggas is buggin'. Fuck I look like stealing from the family? Y'all know me better than that."

Byron's words and nervous laughter made me turn the volume up on my phone.

*"We **knew** you better than that," a familiar voice corrected.*

"Come on, Aura," Byron reasoned. "You know these niggas be on some crab in a barrel type shit. Lie on the next man so they can take his position."

I thought about his lack of accountability and realized it wasn't just with me.

"See, the thing is, I've come across liars, thieves, and fiends in this game. You, my nigga, are all three."

"Come on, Aura. Do..."

POW! POW!

I jumped at the shots and ended the call. I didn't need confirmation that the bullets were for Byron. I was scared but not enough to cry. Fear paralyzed me as I tried to process what I had heard. I was a witness. Although my name wasn't on the scene, my voice held the line. And my connection to the shooter made my stomach turn.

There was only one Aura.

The Aura who'd paid special attention to me. The Aura who'd seen my hidden scars and still decided that I was worth pursuing. He didn't know it yet, but he released me from turmoil and at the same time had me bound by a secret that he didn't know we shared. As my fear slowly turned into relief, tears ran down my cheeks, and my hands pressed together like they had done countless nights before. I'd been praying for God to intervene on my behalf when it came to my relationship.

I was raised to be strong, and as far as the outside world knew, I was. Outside of my home, I didn't take no shit from anyone at any time. So how I ended up in a DV situation was beyond me. I suffered so much, both mentally and physically, being with Byron. While I hadn't prayed for death in this manner, I couldn't lie and say that my prayers didn't end with him having fewer days on Earth. Suddenly, I was free. I didn't need confirmation. Something in my spirit told me I was.

The phone never rang again that night or the nights after. Byron didn't have family that I knew of, and no one ever came looking for him. He was just gone. And I accepted that.

My phone rang in my hand, pulling me back to the present.

Seeing Thyri's name, I answered, ready to seek advice that would help me get my mind right.

"**Hey, boo,**" I greeted in a dull voice.

"**Should I hang up and call back?**" she asked.

"**No.**" I let out a small laugh.

"**You okay?**"

I sighed. "**Honestly, not really.**"

"**Answer your FaceTime.**"

Pulling one of the pillows in front of me, I propped the phone up and accepted the video request. Thyri appeared on the screen, looking freshly fucked with her head wrapped in a silk scarf and her chest partially covered with a comforter.

"**Ummm, what you doing?**" I questioned teasingly.

"**Laying in my bed, nosey. What's wrong?**"

"**Why you ain't got no shirt on?**"

She snickered. "**Cause this my house. I can't be comfortable in my house?**"

"**Why you answering my question wit' a question?**"

"**Why you keep asking me questions?**" she fired back, twisting her neck.

"I'm gonna call you once I make it to the office, aight?"

I heard Enzo's voice clearly before his head popped into the camera. He kissed her a few times, not caring who she was on the phone with. Pulling back, he whispered something in her ear that made her blush and bite her bottom lip. He kissed her once more before turning to the camera.

I waved oddly, making him laugh. "**Heyy.**"

"**Wassup, Danae? You aight?**"

"**Yep.**"

"**Cool. Aye, if that soup Aura made you is nasty, tell that nigga. Don't spare his feelings. I would hate for him to think he can add chef to his list of talents and start bringing shit to the family gatherings for us to try.**"

I laughed and nodded. "**I'll be telling the truth and nothing but the truth.**"

"**Preciate you.**" He stole another kiss from Thyri and disappeared from the camera view.

Thyri's eyes followed him out.

"**Dick got you ready to get in that nigga pocket, don't it?**" I giggled.

"**I'm ready to hang off that man balls, Nae. And you know I've never been the clingy type. Ever.**"

"**I do. But clingy is cool though. As long as you clinging to the right balls, that's alright wit' me.**"

She laughed and sat up straight in the bed, holding the comforter in place. "**My spidey senses tell me they the right balls. You know what else they tell me?**"

"**What?**"

"**That we need to talk.**"

"**We do but not now. I'm in Aura's house.**"

"**Ohhhh.**" Smirking, she nodded. "**And what you doing over there? While you all in my business, that's the question that needs answering.**"

"**Girl, please. As you can see, I'm fully dressed, unlike yourself.**"

"**You are now. Y'all could've been fuckin' all night for all I know.**"

I burst out laughing. "**Well, we were not. With the way my stomach was churning last night, that wouldn't have been going down anyway.**"

I went on to tell her about last night's upset stomach chronicles, Aura arriving unannounced this morning, and how I ultimately ended up in his house.

"**He really don't play 'bout you. Is it over the top? Absolutely. But do I think it comes from a genuine place of care? Absolutely. And you need that, Nae. After all that pain you once carried, it has to feel good to know that someone wants to be the best for you in spite of.**"

"**In spite of what?**"

"**In spite of you standing in your own way.**"

Her words stuck, and this time, I didn't have a comeback. A knock at the door interrupted the silence.

"That's Aura. Let me hit you back when I leave here. Love you."

"Okay, boo. Love you too. And Nae?"

"Yeah?"

"It's okay to give your brain a break for once and just let your heart lead." She flashed me a smile before hanging up.

I closed my eyes, letting her advice sink in, before responding, calling out to Aura to open the door.

He held it open but didn't come in. "How you feeling?"

"Better. Thank you. This mattress is a trap."

"A trap for what?" He chuckled.

"Involuntary sleepovers."

"Girl, ain't nobody tryna kidnap you. Glad to hear you slept well though. I made some soup if you're hungry. And it's good. But if you don't like it, we can order you something."

I smiled. "I'm not really hungry, but I'm gonna eat some because you took the time out to make it."

"Aight. Come on."

Picking up my phone, I followed him out to the kitchen. Wanting to see the food, I walked over to the pot and took the lid off. I nodded my approval. The soup looked hearty, and it smelled amazing. I had high hopes of it tasting just as good.

"If my grandma was here, she would've popped the shit out of you for being in that pot."

"Oh, my bad," I said, placing the lid back on.

He laughed and pulled out a bowl from the cabinet. "You good."

"Here." I held my hand out for the bowl. "I can do it."

He passed it to me, along with a spoon. Ladling the soup into the bowl, I set it on the counter. Positioning himself at the side of me, Aura grinned like he knew something I didn't.

"Why you smiling like that? What you put in here?"

"Girl, you paranoid as hell." He laughed. "We gotta get you in therapy, baby?"

"Shut up. You the one smiling all hard. I ain't even taste it yet."

"I already know it's good. I cooked it with love."

"Mmhmm." I ate a spoonful, and he nodded.

"Shit good, ain't it?"

"You gotta give me a chance to chew and swallow," I said, covering my mouth with my hand.

"By the way you chewing, I already know you savoring the flavors. You ain't gotta tell me what I already know," he replied cockily. "Dada an Aura of all trades."

I ate another spoonful and smirked. "You mean a jack of all trades, crazy."

"Nah. I meant what I said. Ain't no jack here, baby."

"Oh." I giggled. "Whatever you say. This is good though. I gotta give props where props is due."

"Now, that's new for you."

I cut my eye at him. "Don't make me take it back."

"Aight. Aight."

"I would've never pegged you as the cooking type."

"It's a lot of shit I do for the people I love that you don't know about yet. Just imagine when you're my wife. It only gets better."

There it was again, that flutter in my stomach when he mentioned a future for us. I looked down at the bowl, stirring the soup gently. My thoughts drifted to the last thing Thyri said before ending our call. *It's okay to give your brain a break for once and just let your heart lead.* I closed my eyes and took a deep breath, counting to ten before opening them.

When I did, he was staring down at me with a smile tugging at his lips. That alone put me at ease.

"Aura." I said his name as if I didn't already have his attention.

"Danae," he replied, mocking me.

"I wanna ask you something, but it's not something I can just come right out and say."

"That's because women don't usually ask men to marry them,

Ma. It's not the natural order of things." He smiled, and I sucked my teeth.

"Boy, please. I'd drink the water from the Atlantic Ocean through a straw before I ask a nigga hand in marriage. Is you cool?"

He laughed with his hands up. "Just making sure."

"Trust, you don't have to. But on a serious note, I wanna ask you something."

He nodded once, humor fading. "Aight. Go 'head."

"Do you know someone named Byron? He was known in the streets as Banga."

He stilled, and the room went quiet. Not in a way where I felt like he was searching for an answer but more like he was giving me a minute to sit with my question before replying.

"I don't speak on the dead as if they're still present, Ma. So, yes, I **knew** a Banga."

I swallowed hard before asking my next question. "Did you kill him?"

"No. I put a bullet in his head, but he ultimately killed himself."

His honesty should have scared me. Instead, it drew me to him.

"Banga was my ex-boyfriend. The one who liked to box. I was on the phone with him the night he died." I searched Aura's eyes for a reaction and got nothing. "I heard your name and then the shots. And I've been trying to keep my distance ever since. But you, you, Aura Sullivan, just won't leave me alone. You're everywhere. Even in my thoughts although I try my damnedest not to think about you. I figured if I avoided you, then I could somehow erase what happened. But how can I avoid you when you show up time after time? The car for my birthday. The just because flowers. Popping up at the diner to see how my day is going and a host of other shit. How do I embrace you when I know about that night?"

"The same way I embraced you the moment I found out you

were tied to him." The response was simple, but I was having a hard time digesting it.

Placing my hands on the edge of the counter, I tightened my fingers around it. "So, you've known who my ex was this whole time? Did you kill him to prove something to me?" I regretted my question the moment it came out of my mouth. Aura wasn't even that type of nigga. And by the look on his face, I knew he was highly offended.

"Danae, there's a few things you should know about me. I would break a nigga neck if he ever breathed wrong in your presence. I'd shoot a nigga in the face if he looked at you wrong. It don't take much for me. But what I'd never do is kill a nigga behind some pussy that don't belong to me. I didn't know anything about you until that coke-head, thieving ass nigga was dead and gone. And I only looked into you once I decided you were gonna be a permanent fixture in my life."

"Why didn't you say anything?"

"Because I don't make it a habit of holding conversations about other niggas, especially if it ain't no money involved, and I got better shit to talk about."

"Aura, do you not understand that I've been carrying this around? Running from..."

"Me," he said quietly, making my heart ache.

"Running from my feelings. Scared that if you knew that I'd been on the phone that night, you'd see me different. Scared to be open to loving you back because a part of me is still fucked up behind that relationship. And despite the pain it brought me, I feel somewhat guilty for wanting to love you knowing what happened."

His eyes darkened, not with anger but with intense emotion. "First off, you ain't gotta feel guilty 'bout a muthafuckin' thing when it comes to a nigga that didn't give a fuck about your well-being. From today forward, you ain't letting him rent no more space in your head. You know why? Cause you gon' be too busy thinkin' 'bout what country you wanna travel to, what car you wanna drive on a Tuesday, what property you wanna invest in.

And even more important, what colors you want our bridal party to wear for the wedding." He put both hands on my hips and turned my body so that I was fully facing him.

"Aura, I'm scared."

"You don't have to be, Ma. You already experienced the worst version of love. This that good shit over here. And I ain't just talking 'bout the dick I'ma be putting on you."

"Oh, please." I went to push him back, and he pulled me to him by the hem of my blazer.

"Lock in wit' me, Ma. Let me love on you without you pushing me away. I don't care about what you heard or what you witnessed. What I did had to be done. And yes, I'd do it again. It's my job to protect. Whether it be my family or my business, I'ma do that."

"And does protecting me mean I'm dragged more into your world?"

Wrapping his hands around my waist, he leaned in to kiss my forehead. I didn't try to pull back this time.

"I won't drag you. I'll lead from a place of understanding. And if at any point you decide that this is too much for you, I'll free you of me."

I laughed softly. "I just don't see that happening."

"Real shit. I'd hate it, but your happiness means more to me than my need to be the reason you're happy."

His declaration made something shift inside me, and my arms found their way around his neck. Aura towered over me at an even six feet. I stared into his deep brown eyes and allowed myself to fully take him in. To feel for him openly.

"You knew and still loved me anyway. I have so many thoughts in my head that I still need to sort out, but I want to give us a chance. I think..."

I was cut off by him pressing his lips against mine. The kiss was soft, mixed with a hint of balanced aggression.

"You ain't gotta think when I'm around, Nae. Just focus on existing. I got the rest, aight?"

"Okay," I replied, giving my brain a break and letting my heart speak for me.

CHAPTER 10

Keep It A Stack

ENZO

I was leaving my office and headed to Thyri's place when I got a call from Aura, letting me know that Amil had summoned us to the diner. According to him, whatever she wanted to talk about had to be serious because she didn't want to talk over the phone. I figured as much. Amil didn't call family meetings, especially at the diner during the midday rush. If anything, she was clear on the times she didn't want anyone calling her phone unless there was an emergency. If she wanted us both in the same place at the same time, then we did something.

Walking into the diner, I headed straight to the back where Aura was seated. Sliding into the booth, I dapped him up. "What's good? Where Mil at?"

His eyes shifted past me. "She in her office. Told me to text her once you got here."

"Well, I'm here. Text her, nigga."

"Aight," he said but didn't attempt to reach for his phone.

I glanced back over my shoulder to see what had his attention. Only it wasn't a what but a who – Danae. She made her way around the diner, greeting customers, checking on staff, and tending to her managerial duties, while this crazy nigga watched her.

89

I smirked. "Yo' ass is lovesick. Stop staring so hard. That shit creeped out."

He chuckled. "A nigga can't admire his woman in peace?"

"Feel free to stalk when I'm not around, man. You making me uncomfortable."

"Nigga, shut up." He balled up a napkin and tossed it at me. "Nae say she taking a chance on us, but I gotta go at her pace."

I nodded. "That must be some Anderson shit cause Thyri said the same thing."

"And how's that going?"

"She'll be pregnant by spring."

We both cracked up laughing, slapping fives across the table.

"The Sullivan way," he said.

"The only way. About this meeting though. What you think Mil wanna holla at us about?"

"Shit, hell if I know." He shrugged. "I just sent her a text. It better not be about that nigga, Naim, missing. Cause she could've came by the crib for that. This my only chill day."

"You still ain't tell her 'bout that shit?" I asked, referring to Amil's ex, Naim, who Aura had put down a few weeks back.

"Nah. With the holidays, new product drop, and a host of other shit, that wasn't at the forefront of my mind." He reached for the water on the table and took a sip.

I chuckled because killing your sister's man and not telling her would be at the forefront of any normal person's mind. But not Aura's.

"Aye, how I get out this group chat shit with Kyiris? If I get one more memo about this Valentine's Day party, I'ma block her ass on my personal line."

"Yo, the daily reminders she been sending is crazy. Key is a trip."

"Check your phone. She just sent today's update. Now she want a nigga to wear his drawls outside. Fuck is she on?"

"Nigga, what?" I pulled my phone from my pocket to check the text thread. "Man, this say pajama theme. Where you get you gon' be in yo' drawls?" I snickered.

"Shit, that's what I sleep in."

"Well, get ready to be in them cause if I gotta go in there matching pajamas with Thyri, nigga, you betta hit the mall and find you some wit' Danae."

"Yeah, aight, man."

Amil finally appeared minutes later. Stopping at our booth, she crossed her arms on her chest tightly and grilled us.

"What?" Aura spoke first.

"Come to the back," she instructed.

Aura and I shot each other a confused look before getting up from the table and following her to her office.

Inside, Amil stood in the middle of her office, and her eyes bounced between the two of us before speaking. "All I wanna know is where's the body, so I can tell this man aunt something other than I don't know."

Neither of us volunteered to speak, opting to let her question linger for a moment.

"I can't provide that info for you, sis," Aura answered. "His people just gon' have to remember him how he was."

I followed up after his statement. "A goofy, plotting ass nigga."

She sighed and shook her head. Nothing about her reaction gave surprised. Irritated, yes. But not surprised. "I knew something was up once I didn't hear from him for a couple days. But damn, did y'all have to move without giving me a heads up, Aura?"

"What you wanted me to say? Sis, I found out ya nigga was tryna snake me and build his own operation within my shit? And then what you was gon' say?"

"I would've told you to give me some time to feel him out to see what was up."

"And then once you found out what he was up to then what?" I questioned.

She cut her eyes at me. "Don't act like y'all the only ones who bust y'all guns."

"Oh, I know what everybody with the last name Sullivan is

capable of, cousin. The difference in how you would've handled it opposed to how we handled it is clear in your previous statement though. You talkin' bout time to see how a nigga moving. And that's because you don't want it to be true that the person you brought into the fold was on bullshit. Whereas we gon' put a nigga down without hesitation."

"Exactly," Aura agreed. "So, remain as clueless as you are now. And if his people start to lean too hard on you, let me know, and they can go meet him in the upper room. It's really as simple as one, two, three."

She shook her head. "Damn, I really liked him too."

Amil wasn't fucked up about Naim's death. She knew the rules and that everyone under the Sullivan umbrella abided by them, or you ended up missing.

"Oh, yeah? Then, why you ain't bring him to meet Grandma Lettie then?" Aura challenged.

"I said liked, not loved, dummy."

I stood to the side and listened to them go back and forth, same as they did when we were growing up. The shit was comical. But under the irritation and jabs, there was love and respect. And Amil knew that if Aura had to put a nigga down, it was for good reason.

I was about to cut in when my phone chimed. I assumed it was Thyri reaching out to check in. She would text me periodically throughout the day when she had EJ just to keep me in the loop on how his day was going. Even though we were seeing each other, she still took her nanny role serious. What she didn't know was that she would soon be fired with severance pay. I wanted to lock in for the long haul, so there was no need in her working for me anymore.

Pulling my phone from my pocket, I looked down at the screen, and there was a message from Cortez.

> Tez: Unc, you busy right now? I need a huge favor.

Shaking my head, I texted back.

> Me: I'm too busy for bullshit so think about your favor before you ask it.

Three dots appeared on the screen, then another text came through.

> Tez: My assistant principal 'bout to call you. I need you to agree to pick me up. I'll tell you everything once you get here.

My expression shifted, and I knew immediately that Cortez had gotten himself into some bullshit that he didn't want his mother to know about. My cousin, Diane, didn't fuck around. After Cortez's father decided early on that parenthood wasn't a hood he wanted to reside in, she became both mother and father to a four-year-old. And though she had a gang of male cousins, uncles, and a brother that aided in raising him, she still ran a tight ship. Tez knew that, which was why it was my line he hit.

"What happened?" Aura asked, reading my facial expression.

I held my phone up for him to read the message, and he shook his head. There had been plenty of times where we had to pull Tez's collar about how he moved. We'd always cover for him though if we got to him before Diane. It was guy code. We stepped in, got him straight, and sent him back to her once his mind was right.

"That lil' nigga be in more shit than a little bit. Goddamn." Aura huffed.

"Who?" Amil asked.

"None of your business. Nosey ass," Aura responded.

Chuckling, I replied to Cortez, letting him know that I'd be on my way to get him.

"I wasn't even talkin' to you, nigga. Everything straight, E?"

I nodded. "I'm sure it will be. I'ma head out. Love y'all."

"Love you too. And take him witchu." She pointed at Aura, mushing his head.

"Keep yo' hands to yoself before I get my granny on the phone, and it be a problem."

"Nigga, you act like you her only grandchild," she argued.

"I'm her favorite. You know if I call her, she'll get on yo' ass. And I'm chilling here for the day." He walked around her desk and sat in her chair. "Pull the cameras up so I can see my baby."

"That nigga crazy." I laughed, kissing Amil's cheek. "I'ma holla at y'all."

I made my way back out front, waving to Danae as I exited. Hopping in my car, my phone rang. I didn't recognize the number but answered anyway, figuring it was the school.

"Hello?"

A woman's voice came through clearly. **"Hi, is this Enzo Sullivan?"**

"It is."

"Good morning, sir. My name is Crystal Brown. I'm calling from Millenium Prep High School regarding Cortez Sullivan. I've tried contacting his mother, but I've been unsuccessful. Are you a family member?"

"Yes. He's my nephew." Calling Tez my little cousin always seemed weird to me.

"Okay. Well, there's been a situation at the school, and we're requesting a parent or guardian to come in, so we can get things sorted out."

"I can do that. You mind telling me what the situation is? Is he hurt?"

"Oh, no. Of course not. If you don't mind, we'd like to discuss the situation in person rather than on the phone."

"No problem. I'll be there shortly."

"Okay. Thanks. You can come right to the main office once you arrive."

"Got it." The phone beeped with an incoming call from Thyri. I hung up to answer. **"Wassup, Ma?"**

"Hey, are you on your way here?" She sounded flustered.

"You good?" I asked, ignoring her question.

"Yeah. Just a little frustrated. I got a call from KJ's school saying I gotta pick him up. Supposedly there was a situation, but they can't tell me what the hell the situation was."

These two lil' niggas in cahoots, I thought. "I'm headed that way to get Cortez now. I can grab KJ and bring him home. Save you a trip."

"I appreciate it, but I..."

"I gotta come get EJ anyway, remember?"

She paused for a second before responding. "You're right. Let me call the school back and let them know I give them permission for you to get him. I can't believe this."

"Yeah, call them and tell 'em ya man on the way to handle the business."

"Okay." I could hear the smile in her voice, even if it was brief. "Thank you."

"All good. I'll see you in a few."

"K."

Ending the call, I wondered just what the hell these two were up to. Whatever it was, I was going to get the answers before I dropped either of them to their destination.

―――――

THEY WEREN'T FUCKING AROUND WITH SECURITY AT Millenium Prep. Before I could enter the building, I had to scan my ID then have it checked by school safety. It felt more like I was going to visit a damn prison than a school. I was all for security, but goddamn, was this Eastside High? By the time I was escorted to the main office, I didn't care about what Tez or KJ had done. I was ready to go.

"Good morning. How can I help you?" An older Black woman with a stern face that looked like she gave the students hell greeted me.

"Good morning, I'm here for Cortez Sullivan and Kaleb Smith."

She glanced down at a book in front of her then back up at me. "You're here to get them both?"

"I am," I replied evenly.

"Right this way," she said, walking around the counter she stood behind.

I didn't know who mama this lady was, but there had to be an old nigga happy as hell somewhere because she was thick. The face gave forty-two, but the body didn't look no older than thirty-two. I wasn't on the market, but a nigga had eyes.

We entered a small hallway then walked into an office labeled principal. Inside the office, KJ and Cortez were seated off to the side with their coats on, bookbags in their laps, and solemn looks on their faces. A familiar face sat behind a medium-sized oak desk. On the desk was an acrylic sign that read Principal Malcolm.

"Thank you, Ms. Reed," he said to the woman as she exited.

The door closed, and the principal stood to his feet with his hand extended to me. "Not too many Sullivans come across my desk these days, so to find out Cortez is one of yours was a surprise."

"Well, you know we don't travel in packs, and we're often seen before we're heard, Tim."

"Yeah, he got that slick talk honestly. Wassup, man?"

We shook hands and embraced in a brotherly hug. I knew Timothy Malcolm from high school. We were on a travel basketball team together. Niggas hated him because he was undisputedly the best player on the team and dominated the court. I, on the other hand, didn't care. I played my position well and never let another nigga shining dim my light. And that was where we bonded – our tendency to not give a fuck and being ready to throw hands with anybody on the team that wanted static.

"I ain't seen you in years, man. A principal? Who would've ever thought."

He sat on the edge of his desk. "Not me." He chuckled. "But here I am. Making sure my kids are learning and making smart decisions. Even if I gotta hit 'em with that tough love. Ain't that right, fellas?"

We both looked over at the boys, who shifted uncomfortably in their seats. KJ's shoulders were hunched over, while Tez avoided eye contact altogether.

"So, wassup? Why am I here?"

He pulled a colorful package from the pocket of his suit jacket and handed it to me. Upon close inspection, I knew it was a Za bag. I was hot, but I played it cool.

"So, they had this on them?" I asked.

Tim folded his arms across his chest with a tight expression, on some real principal shit. "No. They didn't have it on them, but these bags have been floating around the school the last two weeks, along with their names."

"So, they in here off the strength of hearsay?" I followed up, hoping that he wasn't on no bullshit like that.

"I brought them in to see what they knew."

"Like an interrogation?"

"No. Like a conversation. I wanted to give them both the benefit of the doubt. As I mentioned, their names have been the ones linked to the distribution of these packs."

Although I knew they were likely behind what was going on, I didn't like that it was being implied without evidence of them making a sale.

"See, that word distribution implies that they're actually making sales. Again, something you have no knowledge of but have heard rumors about. Copy. You then have the parents called to come down here and do what, Mr. Malcolm?" My tone had shifted to something serious.

"I figured we all could get down to the bottom of this together by making a collaborative effort to find out what the boys know."

"Bet." I turned back to them with the bag held up in the air. "Y'all selling this shit on school grounds?"

"Nah," Cortez answered first, and KJ echoed his statement. "Nah."

I could see the look of disappointment on Tim's face when I turned back to him. "So, what now?"

"I'm not so sure."

"Yeah, you gon' have to give me more than that cause I'm not feeling them being reprimanded for something you're not sure about. So, while you figure that out, I'ma take them home for the day. Let you sleep on it. But they'll be back tomorrow. And if for any reason you feel they shouldn't return tomorrow, you can let me know, and I'll have my attorney contact the superintendent to find out the best way to proceed."

By the way his forehead creased, I knew he wasn't feeling my response. Nodding slowly, he held his hand out again for me to shake.

"We'll see them tomorrow."

"Sounds good." I handed him back the bag and turned to the boys. "Let's go."

Cortez practically jumped up from his seat, relief written all over his face, like he'd gotten away with something. Little did he know, I was gon' get on his ass as soon as we hit the parking lot. KJ stood slower, tense. He knew he wasn't in the clear yet. Unlike Cortez, he still had to deal with his mother.

I walked ahead of the two out of the office and into the hallway.

"Unc, we..."

"Don't speak, Cortez," I said, keeping my eyes straight ahead.

He went quiet immediately. We walked out of the building in silence, and I didn't speak until we were in the car. I didn't bother starting it up before my gaze landed on Cortez first.

"You deadass?"

"What?" He played stupid, and I punched him in his chest. "Ahhh." He hunched over in pain.

"Play dumb and I'ma box yo' ass right in this car." We were always tough on the boys in our family. Everybody got beat the fuck up and loved on in the end. It was a balance that made us Sullivan men. "Why you out here moving stupid? Correction, why y'all out here moving stupid?" I cut my eyes back at KJ in the rearview mirror. "Y'all out here selling Za bags like y'all some corner niggas. Fuck is going on?"

"It ain't ours," KJ said with a straight face.

"Bullshit. I ain't the one y'all need to lie to. If you gon' keep it a stack wit' anybody, it need to be me, so I can help y'all find a way outta this shit."

KJ's facial expression changed to one of hope. I knew he ain't want smoke with Thyri just as much as Tez ain't want it with his mama.

"We ain't even sell it," Tez spoke up. "We was just showing it to our people to show that we had it."

Another lie. I leaned back in my seat and forced my tone down into something steadier. "So, you want me to believe that y'all showing off weed packs for shits and giggles? Cut the bull-shit, Cortez."

"We sold a few packs," KJ finally admitted.

Cortez's head whipped in his direction. "Man, what the fu..."

"Shut up," I scolded him. "He ain't tellin' me shit I ain't already know."

Starting up the car, I pulled out of the parking lot and headed to Cortez's house first.

"We weren't even selling to anyone outside our circle." Cortez spoke after we'd been riding for a few minutes. "Can't even trust niggas to hold it down."

"You sound real stupid, you know that?" I glanced over at him, and his jaw clenched. "Yeah, lil' nigga, get mad. You talkin' 'bout y'all only sold to y'all circle. It don't matter who you sold that shit to. You sold it on school grounds. You know who the fuck your family is, and you out here sellin' bum ass Za packs? And you," I looked back at KJ again. "You ain't exempt from this shit either. Only thing is I can't put my hands on you. But y'all pulled this dumb ass move for what? Sneaker money? Pocket money? Shit that y'all get without even asking? Make that make sense. Better yet, answer the number one question. Where y'all get it from?"

Neither spoke, both of their heads turning toward the window at the same time.

"Don't make me ask again."

"My uncle," KJ uttered.

"Yo' uncle gave you weed to sell, bruh?"

"Nah. He gave it to me to smoke. I decided to sell it. Cortez really ain't have nothing to do wit' it. He just was..."

"Helping him sell it," Cortez jumped in, letting me know in not so many words that he wasn't letting his man go down by himself.

It was admirable, but it didn't change the fact that they still fucked up. I eased onto Cortez's block and pulled up in front of his building. Turning off the engine, I turned to him before he could run out of my car.

"Let me explain something to both of y'all. Leave the street shit for the niggas that belong in them. Don't be the ones trying so hard to be a part that y'all start doing goofy shit like this and put a target on y'all back."

"It was just weed, Unc," Cortez tried to reason like it was no big deal.

"Weed today, coke tomorrow. Y'all got so much shit going for yourselves. Popular, talented, handsome young niggas but y'all wanna do bum shit like sell weed. If y'all wanna be the talk of Millenium Prep, do it for some playa shit. This ain't it."

"Aight, Unc. We hear you." Cortez had his hand on the door handle like he was ready to go.

"I'm sure you don't, but it's cool. Just know there's consequences for your actions. I'll be hittin' yo' line with that consequence after I drop him off."

He huffed and sucked his teeth as he opened the passenger side door. "I'ma hit when I can, KJ. Hold ya head." Reaching in the backseat, he dapped KJ up.

"He ain't going to prison, bruh. You talkin' bout hold ya head. Getcho dramatic ass outta here. Hop in the front, KJ."

I waited until Cortez walked into his building before pulling off.

"My moms asked you to come get me?" KJ inquired.

"Nah. I offered since I was already coming for Tez. That cool witchu?"

He shrugged. "It's cool. Was she mad when you spoke to her?"

"Flustered," I replied. "I think she was more worried than anything."

"Man, she ain't gon' let me out her sight now." He shook his head. "Then I know she gon' tell my pops. I'ma just go in the crib, hand her my phone, unplug my game, the PC, and hand her that too."

The stress was clear in his voice.

"Was Cortez with you when your uncle gave you the weed?" He slouched in the seat and played with his twist. That gesture alone, followed by him diverting his eyes from me, let me know he was about to lie. "Nah."

"Aye," I tapped his chest, "you can lie to me but do yourself a favor and don't go in there and lie to your moms. From what I see, you're a good kid. Tez is too. Y'all just do stupid shit from time to time. But understand this. When you start partaking in adult shit, you gotta be ready for them adult consequences. And you may not wanna hear this, but that was some lame ass shit yo' uncle did." I could've kept the last part of my sentence to myself, but I couldn't let that shit ride.

He didn't reply, and I understood why. Whether right or wrong, Koric was his blood. And even when the truth about someone you loved hurt, it didn't make it easier to hear. Part of me respected his silence. The other part felt like he needed to sit with that truth.

We arrived at his house, and he didn't attempt to reach for the door handle when I parked.

"Look, so long as you're honest and don't try to sugarcoat what happened, I'll be right there witchu, so she won't go too hard on you."

"Maannnn, my mother wouldn't care if you were Jesus Christ himself. If she need to get on my ass, she gon' get on my ass. You being her boyfriend ain't stoppin' nothing."

I chuckled. "You might be right. But look, I can make a

suggestion for a punishment that don't keep you locked in the house. How that sound?"

He frowned. "It sounds like you tryna use this situation to get in good wit' me."

I went to break the news to him that I wasn't the nigga that longed for anyone's approval, then he cracked a smile and sat up straight in the seat.

"It's working. What you need me to do?"

I couldn't help but burst out laughing. "Bruh, get out my car. You on yo' own to face the music now."

I got out, and he followed behind me. "Nah, Enzo. Tell me what I need to do. I ain't tryna be on house arrest, man."

"We'll see."

At the door, he fumbled with his keys, unknowingly giving it away that he had fucked up.

"Stop shaking, Za man," I joked. "I got you," I said, placing my hand on his shoulder and giving it a reassuring squeeze. "Open the door."

Sticking his key in the lock, he went to turn it, and the door was pulled open. Thyri stood on the other side of it with EJ on her hip and sharp eyes peering into KJ's soul as only a mother could.

"What happened?" she asked.

KJ glanced back at me like I was the one she was questioning.

"Let's go inside," I suggested.

She stepped back to let us in, and something in me said that this moment would be one of the many moments that would shape the way we navigated this relationship.

CHAPTER 11

Let's Be Clear

THYRI

The door closed behind KJ and Enzo, and I felt the heat rolling up my spine. I was pissed off. Shifting EJ to my other hip, I stared KJ down so hard, you would've thought I had X-ray vision. His eyes landed everywhere but my face. He stood still and didn't bother walking to his room. That alone let me know that whatever happened was worse than I thought.

"So, what happened at school?" I asked again.

KJ didn't answer. Instead, he glanced back at Enzo like he was searching for a lifeline. I followed his gaze and caught the reassuring head nod Enzo threw his way. Still, nobody was talking.

"Enzo don't go to Millenium Prep, Kaleb. I'm not looking for answers from him. You need to tell me something because the silence is making it easy for me to come up with my own answers. Neither of us want that."

The air tightened in the room, and I went to step toward KJ. Enzo moved in sync with me. It wasn't a quick step. Nor was it threatening or commanding. It was intentional and protective. He crossed in front of KJ to me. Gently lifting EJ from my hip, he pressed his lips to my forehead and whispered, "Not in front of me, Ma."

The gentleness in his tone settled me, like he was reminding me that we were still new and he wanted to respect that this was a conversation that me and KJ needed to have alone. Exhaling through my nose, I caught on.

"Go to your room, KJ. I'll be right there."

He moved quickly, almost tripping over his own feet.

"EJ's oatmeal is cooling on the counter. He has a fruit cup and his juice in the fridge. This one has the fruit in water instead of syrup. I don't know if he'll like it but try it out."

Enzo nodded once. "I got it, baby. And if it means anything, I had a conversation with KJ on the ride here. If I overstepped, I apologize in advance."

I smiled. "No need to apologize. I appreciate it. I'm gonna apologize in advance though. If you hear some furniture moving back there, it's just me boxing with KJ."

"Mannn." He laughed. "Go on, woman."

Smirking, I turned around and made my way to KJ's bedroom. Pushing the cracked door open, I disregarded the clutter and focused on him. Closing the door behind me, I stood a few feet from where he sat on the edge of his bed, staring straight ahead.

"Talk."

He shifted on the bed then swallowed before speaking. "I'm not suspended."

"That's good to hear. It still doesn't explain why you're in my house at eleven in the morning when you should be at them people school. So, again, I ask what... the... hell happened?"

I watched his chest rise and fall as he sighed loudly. "I was called into the principal's office about some weed being sold around the school."

"And?"

"That's it," he said quickly.

"Do you want me to wring your goddamn neck, Kaleb?"

"No."

"So, stop playin' wit' me. Were you selling weed?"

"Yeah. But..." His ringing phone cut him off.

I knew it was his father calling by the ringtone.

"Answer it," I pushed.

"Ma..."

"I said pick up the phone," I repeated through gritted teeth. "And put it on speaker."

He dropped his head and pulled the phone from his pocket to answer.

"Wassup, son?" Kaleb's voice came through light.

"Wassup, Pop?" KJ responded, sounding like he'd lost his best friend.

"Wassup witchu? Why you sound all down and shit?"

"Our son has something he needs to tell you," I said, refusing to play KJ's game of mum's the word.

"Thyri?" He called out my name, clearly confused. **"Where y'all at? It's the middle of the school day."**

"It's funny you say that. Tell him where you are and why you're here, weed man."

KJ's head dropped and for good reason. Dealing with me was one thing but dealing with his father was a whole other beast.

"I got picked up early."

"For?"

"It damn sure ain't because he had an appointment," I said. KJ cut his eye in my direction and shook his head.

"What were you picked up for, Kaleb?"

KJ's voice cracked. **"I was called into the principal's office today. Word around the school is I've been selling weed."**

"Dawg, ain't no way you just said that to me," Kaleb let out in a low tone before a roar. **"Ain't no way you went out and did the shit that we just talked about you not fucking doing the last time, KJ. Fuck is up witchu?"**

KJ's leg jumped up and down, while he pulled at the skin on his lip. I thought back to the heated back and forth I'd walked in on last month between the two and began to connect the dots. Kaleb had made it clear then that he had handled the situation, so there was no need for me to know anything. Whatever the issue was, KJ was to stay clear of the projects for a while. Something in my gut told me that this whole weed selling thing had something to do with that conversation. So, I asked the question that I was sure Kaleb and his son knew the answer to.

"Where'd you get the weed from, KJ?"

He kept his eyes on the phone in his hand and rubbed the back of his neck. "I got it from Uncle Koric."

I sucked in a breath and pressed my lips tightly together to keep from flipping the fuck out. Kaleb went quiet on the other end of the phone, so quiet that I thought he'd muted because I didn't even hear him breathing. That lasted a few seconds before his voice came back, controlled.

"Yo, unplug every game system in that room, PC included. Give the phone to your mother and I'll get back to you in a minute."

I didn't give KJ a chance to move before I stepped forward and snatched the phone from his hand. "Put everything in the hallway once it's disconnected."

"Alright."

Turning, I walked out. I stepped out into the hallway with the phone pressed against my ear.

"Tyri!" EJ squealed while bolting toward me.

"Gimme a second, Kaleb," I said, crouching down to catch EJ in my arms. I kissed the top of his head. "I'll be right out, okay? Go to Daddy."

I pointed behind him where Enzo had started to walk down the hall.

"My bad, Ma. I got him," Enzo said quietly, taking EJ by the hand.

I held my hand up to him and pointed to the phone. He understood immediately, turning and walking back to the living room, giving me privacy without me having to ask. I stepped into my bedroom and brought the phone back to my ear, closing the door behind me.

"Who you got in the house?"

My face scrunched up, stopping mid-step.

"The only person that concerns you in this house is a

junior. You haven't been asking who's here. Don't start now."

"I don't ask because..."

"You don't reserve that right. You're KJ's father. Not mine. I don't get questioned."

He exhaled heavily. I knew he was tight, but that wasn't my problem.

"Cool. I'll deal with Koric and talk to KJ." He attempted to end the conversation because he was in his feelings, but this wasn't the time for him to let his ego override the co-parenting that we agreed to.

"I let you just brush me off the last time, Kaleb, but not this time. We need to come together to handle this. Your brother gave our son weed. What the hell is that about? Is he tryna recruit my son to be his little block boy? Cause that shit ain't happenin'."

"I don't know what the fuck Koric got going on." Frustration bled through his tone, but I wasn't fazed by it. "I won't know until you let me get off the phone to handle it."

"And then what? I should trust that you'll call me back to let me know what's going on or go around me so long as you feel it's handled?"

"Man, I ain't got time to be going back and forth wit' you. Tend to your company and I'll take care of what's going on with our son."

"Our son, nigga," I shot back. "Don't be so deep in your feelings that you forget that."

He ended the call without responding. I wasn't about to coddle Kaleb when I had a fifteen-year-old weed dealer in the other room. While he was handling things with his brother, I was going to be brainstorming punishments for KJ that would keep him so busy he wouldn't even have time to miss a game system because his ass was going to be dog tired.

I returned to the living room to find Enzo instructing EJ on how to put on his own coat. EJ was half cooperating, distracted by some cartoon playing on the TV screen. Enzo was patient as ever, having him put one arm in and then the other.

"There you go, big man," he said once EJ finally got it right.

As I walked around the couch, he glanced up at me. He didn't say anything at first, just stared at me like he was looking for a sign to move. I sat on the arm of the couch and rolled my shoulders back to release some of the tension in them. Whatever he saw on my face must've been enough because he stepped toward me, closing the distance between us. Standing in front of me, he placed his hands on both sides of my cheeks and lifted my face.

"You aight?" he asked.

I nodded once. My silence must've told him I needed more than just a verbal check in. I needed physical touch. Enzo reached for me and pulled me up from the couch and into his arms. Resting my head on his shoulder, I let the weight of the day settle there, even though it wasn't even noon yet.

For a second, I allowed myself to lean on a man again, and Enzo held me tight. Closing my eyes briefly, I heard a small grunt. Opening them, I giggled, seeing a determined EJ pushing himself off the couch and running over. Planting himself between us, he tried his hardest to wrap his little arms around both of our legs at once.

"You don't let Daddy get a minute when you around, huh?" Enzo said, lifting him up.

EJ grinned like he knew he'd gotten his way.

"He just want some love too," I cooed, kissing EJ's forehead. "Thanks again for getting KJ for me."

"No thanks needed. I think you handled the situation well. I'm glad you didn't talk to him in front of me either. I used to hate when my mama did that shit. I even bring it up to her today. It's cool that you didn't embarrass him. But you ain't let him slide either."

"Yeah. It's never my goal to break him down. Especially in front of other people. We gon' get an understanding though.

There's no way around that. Quick question, do you have any cleaning jobs this weekend?"

"There's always work to be done. Why, wassup?"

"I wanted to see if KJ could go on a job. I need a punishment, and we've been through the whole taking the phone and game thing before, and I don't think it's effective. I want him to work."

"Oh, we can most definitely make that happen. I'm putting Cortez ass to work too. Since they wanna be Cheech and Chong."

I wasn't surprised to hear that Cortez was in on it. He and KJ had been like Siamese twins lately.

"To find out that it was his uncle that gave him the weed makes it worse. I'm concerned that KJ is becoming too easily influenced, and I can't have that."

"Yeah. I told him that that wasn't cool at all on his uncle's part. As far as influence, at that age, it's nothing but a constant reminder that everybody ain't meant to be in the streets. Ain't nothing appealing about it except for the money. And as fast as you get that shit in, it goes right back out. They gon' be aight though. I guarantee it." He kissed my lips and then my forehead. "You wanna put him in the Sullivan scared straight program?"

"The what?" I laughed.

"I'm just fuckin' witchu. Just wanted to see you smile again. Me and EJ gon' slide though, so y'all can have the rest of the day to sort things out. I'm gonna get with the cleaning crew booked this weekend and see what they have on the schedule."

"Okay, thank you. Come give me a hug, EJ. You leaving me." I walked over to him and fake pouted.

"Tyri sad?" he said, looking up at me.

"A little bit." I hugged him and kissed his cheek. "You be back soon?"

"I back," he replied, and Enzo laughed.

"I'll take your word for it." Picking him up, I carried him to the door. "Text me when you make it in," I told Enzo.

"Will do."

I let them out, locking the door behind them. Making my way down the hall, I stopped in front of KJ's bedroom door and stood there. There was no doubt that I was disappointed in him, but I wasn't going to let this incident define his future. If I had to constantly redirect him, I would. If I had to monitor his movements, I'd do that too. If it was one thing I was clear on, it was the fact that I'd take KJ out of here before I let the streets have him.

CHAPTER 12

Right Where You Want Me

DANAE

"Y'all get home safe," I said to the duo who had come in at eleven thirty, just before the kitchen closed, to have the diner's famous French toast.

The kitchen closed at midnight, and although they were cutting it close, the chef still made it do what it do. The French toast was fluffy, stuffed with cream cheese and your choice of fruit compote on top. Amil made sure that at Sullivan's, you had the overall diner experience, but elevated. The food was consistent whether you came in at 8 a.m. when it opened or just before closing. Ingredients were fresh and cooked to perfection.

"You too. And thanks again." The women waved and left out.

"Alright, y'all. It's time for me to head out too," Chef Bee said, walking out front, dressed in her street clothes. She was also a Sullivan.

"Night, Bee," Aura said from where he sat at the back of the diner. "Love you. Text me when you make it home."

"Okay." She hugged me and whispered, "My cousin so crazy 'bout you."

"Girl, good night." I giggled and pushed the door open to let her out.

Locking it behind her, I flipped the sign from open to closed. Turning, I found Aura walking in my direction. The man had

111

really spent the whole day at the diner with me. He didn't hover or interrupt as promised, just stayed present, watching from a distance. I'd never met a man so enthralled with me. No one had ever wanted to be in my presence as much as Aura did. And honestly, I was soaking it all in.

"You worked yo' ass off today," he said.

"I work my ass off every day," I corrected. "I can't believe you spent your whole day here. A businessman like yourself ain't have nothing better to do?" I grinned, leaning against the booth, while he stood across from me.

"I couldn't think of anything better to do today than to watch you. Plus, when you're the boss, the money is wherever you are, so I made money while watching you. I think the day went pretty well."

"And who am I to argue a valid point?"

He smirked. "What else you gotta do before you head out?"

I cocked my head to the side. "You mean what else **we** gotta do? Since you're here, I could use your help. Two heads are better than one."

His lips curled into a smile. "You know, when I think about head, that phrase never comes to mind."

"Oh, my God." I picked the checkbook up front the table and hit him with it. "Shut up, nasty. The faster you help me, the faster we can go. Can you put the chairs up on the tables, so maintenance can come in and do their thing?"

"I can do whatever you want me to if you let me put my lips on yours."

"Okay," I agreed without pressure. I could tell it shocked him. But he made it easy to give in tonight just by keeping his word.

Stepping forward, he reached out and pulled me to him. It was quick. Possessive in a way. I liked it. He lifted my head with his finger and kissed my lips twice.

"I like that glossy shit," he said, smiling and kissing me again. When he ran his nose along my bottom lip, I giggled. "Coconut." He picked up on the scent then kissed me a fourth time.

A wide grin spread across my face, and goosebumps crept up

the back of my neck. This was the kind of flirty, goofy, loving attention I'd longed for in previous relationships. Most men didn't display this kind of adoration. Aura, on the other hand, didn't hide it.

"You just want me to put the chairs up?" he asked once he'd gotten his fix.

"Yes, please. You can start at the back. I'm gonna run the register, and we can head out after."

"Aight." Slowly releasing me, he stepped back and got to work.

We caught a groove in the silence – me counting, him putting up the chairs. It didn't take long for him to complete the task since the diner only had a few two and four top tables. Once he was done, he sat down at the counter, while I finished noting the day's earnings.

"You still thinking about doing the Airbnb hosting?"

I nodded. "Yeah. I've researched a few neighborhoods, pricing, and properties to see what will make the most profit. I'm not as diligent as I could be, but I'm gonna change that."

"What's stopping you from being diligent?"

"Money." I giggled like that wasn't obvious. "And the fact that I want what I want. And that requires more money than I have right now for the areas I'm looking to rent in."

"Money is easily attainable," he said.

"Says the boss."

"The boss that you're attached to."

"Ughh. Aura, don't be that guy."

He frowned. "What guy?"

"The one that flaunts his money in the relationship. The one that uses it as a flex to show a woman what he can do for her. It's corny."

He smirked. "You think I do that? You think I'm tryna flex when I buy you things?"

I thought about how meaningful the gifts were that he'd bought me, my car being the biggest one. There was always a "just because" note or text attached to it. Maybe I was contradicting myself. "I mean, no. It's just the way you said that. It was just... eeeyuck." I mimicked the TikTok creator, Ariana.

"Money is a tool, so I use it as such. According to my grandmother, my love language is acts of service. It's been that way since I was a kid. Your car wasn't a flex. I just wanted to see you in something different. The flowers, jewelry, and all-expense paid maintenance days are things I feel you deserve. So, I have no problem doing that. When I say money is attainable because you have access to me, it's not cause I'm tryna pop it. I say it because as my woman, you being taken care of and not having to think about where the money's coming from cause Dada got it is the flex. I don't have to say I'm the boss, Nae. That shit so embedded in me, I walk with a boss air."

By the time he finished talking, my nipples were hard, and my panties were wet. It wasn't just what he said, it was how he said it. Aura Sullivan was exactly who the fuck he thought he was and then some.

"I hear you," I finally spoke while squeezing my legs together behind the register. "I guess you can say I'm just trying to figure this out on my own, ya know? You get a different kind of satisfaction when you know you put the work in yourself."

"I respect that 100%. I never wanna take away from your grind. I do have a proposition for you that doesn't include you being on all fours." He winked, and I pondered with heavy consideration.

"And what's that?" I asked instead of saying what was really on my mind.

"What if I become a silent investor for you? We can start with two properties. The reason I say two is because you wanna have options. One that's affordable but still gives the guest the feeling of luxe by the way you decorate and then one that's more high end. It comes with additional services such as transportation for the duration of their time in the Airbnb and offers full clean up at no expense to them once their stay ends. Of course, it'll be more costly, but you'll get bookings. It's all in how you upsell. People gotta get around. Once you reach your first 5k, you can start putting the money in our wedding account. How that sound?"

I stuffed the money as well as the receipts into the bank pouch and put it under my arm. "It sounds great. I couldn't think of a thing wrong until you mentioned our wedding."

"What about it?"

Setting the bag down, I walked around the counter and sat on the stool next to him. "You put so much stake in me, Aura, that it makes me wonder. Have you ever been in love?"

"I'm Aura, baby. I exude love and shit." He smiled.

I shook my head, letting out a small laugh. "No, seriously. Have you ever been in love?"

He stared at me for a few seconds before answering. "I can't say that I have."

I didn't believe him. "Seriously?"

He shook his head. "I've dealt with women but never at the level where I was open to giving them my heart."

"Did you feel they didn't deserve it?"

"I'm sure a few of them did. I've just never been open to giving it... until you."

"Why?" Just like he was persistent in pursuing me, I was the same with my questions.

"I watched my father love my mother with everything he had. I grew up watching him display the kind of love that made the room feel light if it was tense when she walked in because his love moved with her." He paused.

It seemed like something he'd sat with for a while that he wanted to get out, so I stayed quiet, giving him space to reflect as he spoke.

"I always felt that kept her grounded. Kept her present. But it didn't. She was fighting an internal battle with herself, and although she allowed my father to love her, she never let him get in the ring to fight alongside her. My mother killed herself when I was thirteen. I watched what it did to my pops in real time. He's moved on since then, but I don't think his heart ever recovered.

From thirteen, I said that I would never give a woman that kinda access to me."

"So, essentially, you withheld your heart to avoid being hurt."

"Yes," he admitted. "I gave women what they wanted physically, time, money, attention, and dick to compensate for what I couldn't give them."

I was searching for the right words to say but came up blank.

"And then you made me work."

"What I made you work for?"

"You." His words landed soft but solid. "You did your best to avoid my attention. You didn't ask for my time or money, and I couldn't talk you into a date, let alone drop dick in you."

I laughed because one thing about it, I was hard on a nigga after Byron. "I have been ducking and dodging, huh?"

"Like a muthafucka." He chuckled.

"So, is that why you wanna give me your heart? Because I made you chase me?"

He stood and closed the small distance between us. "I wanna give it to you because you don't ask for it. You've never chased for anything I've given you. Shit, I gotta chase you down to give it." We both laughed. "Nobody challenges me the way you do, Danae. And a man of my caliber doesn't want someone I can easily conquer."

He pressed his forehead against mine, and all of a sudden, I was overcome with emotion. *Bitch, you better not cry,* I thought as I felt tears welling up in my eyes. This was too much. This was too real. Too raw.

"Aura." I whispered his name and breathed through my nose.

"Stay right here with me. Here and now. I'm giving you permission to take my heart as yours to keep. I know you're the one for me. My granny kept you in prayer for me. Be a nigga safe space, Nae. I'll take care of everything else. If I'm anything, I'm a man of my word. Will you take my heart?"

He placed his hands on my jaw to cup my face.

"Yes," I replied lowly. "I'll take your heart, Aura. And I'll trust you with mine." My heart galloped, then I kissed him.

He responded immediately, wrapping his arms around my waist and pulling me up from the stool. The kiss deepened, and his hands found their way to my ass. Palming both cheeks, he slipped his tongue in my mouth, and what was meant to be a kiss to solidify our exchange of hearts became more passionate. Aura's hands found their way under my blazer where he caressed my back lovingly.

"Mmmm," I moaned into his mouth while bringing my hand up to the back of his neck. I wanted – no, I needed – him so bad.

He must've heard my inner thoughts because the next thing I knew, he lifted me up and set me on the counter. "You bout to gimme this pussy right here on this counter," he let out, his voice laced with passion.

"We can't, Aura. That's disrespectful as hell." My mouth said one thing, but the way my pussy was throbbing said another.

"I'll pay to get it cleaned, baby. I promise." His lips found my neck, kissing and dragging his tongue across it.

"Mmmmm, sssss. She has cameras in here, Auraaa."

He didn't stop his tongue assault but managed to speak in between kisses. "You... (muah) ... better ... (muah) ... show (muah) ... out then (muah)."

After the last kiss, I said fuck it. I needed him, and he was going to have me with or without my say so. As he tended to my neck, I pulled off my blazer. I didn't fully get my arm out of my left sleeve before he ripped my shirt open. Buttons were every-where, evidence of the height of our passion. The move was sexy, but once I came down from the high, I was sure that I was going to remember that he ripped my favorite button up from Banana Republic. I came out of the shirt, and he went to pull my titty out my bra.

I giggled lowly. "Wait, bae," I said, gently pushing him back. This was a good lace set from Savage x Fenty.

He paused. "What?"

"It unsnaps in the front. Look." I unclasped the bra, and my titties popped out, all perky and ready to be sucked.

"That shit sexy as hell," he expressed before sticking out his tongue and twirling it around my right nipple.

"Ooouuu," I crooned in pure ecstasy. My hands were flat on the counter to hold me up as I threw my head back.

Aura gave both nipples equal attention, alternating from licking to sucking them. My body was on fire. Any other night, foreplay would've been a must, but I was too horny to wait for the main event.

"I need you inside me, Aura."

He didn't wait for any further instruction. He unbuttoned my slacks, and I lifted up so that he could pull them off, along with my panties, kicking my shoes off simultaneously. I opened my legs wide, and the heat radiated off my sex. Aura stepped back and admired my bald pussy. When he kneeled down eye level and started to speak to it, it further confirmed that this man was insane.

"I've waited a long time to meet you. Accept Dada with open arms when I get inside, aight? We gotta get well acquainted because I'll be seeing you more frequent than you expect. You so damn pretty too." He gave my pussy a wet kiss then a light slap that made me quiver.

With lust filled eyes, I watched as he dropped his jeans to his ankles. And oh, the dick. The dick was magical, at least seven and a half inches in length. It was a shade darker than his face and just beautiful. He stroked it twice before placing it at my opening. My juices seeped out of me as he swiped his dick up and down my slit.

"Mmmmm, condom, Aura," I said just as he slid into me slowly. "Ahhhhh." My head dropped back, and my mouth hung open as he fed me inch by inch until he was deep inside of me.

I felt his hands around my throat as he thrust into me. "Look at me, Danae. Let me see those beautiful eyes." I squeezed my pussy muscles, and his hand tightened around my neck. "Sssss. Ooouu, shit. You starting already, huh? Put your head up and look at me."

"Ughhhh, Auraaaa." The way he grinded into me, coupled with his hand around my throat, took me to higher heights and deeper depths. "Ohhhh, you better do that shit, Daddy," I cried out, moving my hips to match his rhythm. "You got me so fuckin' wet. Ughhhh."

He squeezed a little harder and twisted his hips so that he had easy access to my A spot. That got me to lift my head and look in his eyes like he requested, not because I was afraid that he would choke me out but because I knew he didn't count on me fucking back.

"Ooouuu, yesss. You doing that pussy so good. Keep it right there, baby."

"Right here, Mama?" He sped up his strokes, hittin' that spot, making my eyes roll in the back of my head. "Tell Dada what make his better half feel good. When that dick hit that spot like that?"

"Ooohhh, fuck. I'm cumming."

He lifted me from the counter and bounced me up and down on his dick. "Wet that dick up for me cause I'm 'bout to bust," he said in my ear, and that did it.

I came hard. "Auraaaaa."

"Shitttt. I'm cummin' too, baby." I could feel him pulsating inside me and painting my walls. I didn't regret one minute.

He kissed all over my face while carefully walking me back over to the counter and setting me down. "If we did all that in here, I know damn well that we'll fuck up a bed."

I still had my arms wrapped around his neck, trying to regulate my breathing. "I really hope Amil never looks at the tape for today. She's gonna kill me. Maybe even fire me." I shook my head.

Aura pulled the hair from my face and laughed. "You good, baby. If she ever sees this footage, she'll cuss me out and have one of those *yessss, bitch* moments with you. But if you get fired, it was worth it, right?"

"Aura!" I pulled away from him and punched him in his chest.

"I'm just playing. Gimme kiss."

I kissed him twice. "Let me get down so I can get dressed." I clasped my bra back and hopped down off the counter. "And we gotta find the buttons to this shirt. And clean down the counter. I can't believe you ripped my favorite shirt." I put my blazer on and held the shirt up to him.

"My bad, baby," he said, pulling his pants up. "I was in the moment and always wanted to do that shit. It just seemed like the perfect time."

I snickered. "Something is really wrong with you. You owe me a new shirt." I stepped into my pants and sneakers.

"Come here." He beckoned me forward with his finger.

I walked to him with a smile.

"You know I got you." His put his lips on mine and kissed me.

My head rested on his chest, and I felt his heartbeat.

"It recognizes you," he murmured.

"Yeah? How you know that?" I questioned, keeping my head in place.

"Because it's settled."

I stayed still and secretly promised that I would remain right where he wanted me and take care of the heart he'd entrusted to me.

CHAPTER 13

The Sullivan Approach

AURA

I'd been on a high the last couple days since becoming acquainted with Danae's cervix. It felt like home as soon as I slid inside her, further solidifying that she was made for me. My life didn't allow me to float in my feelings for days, not when the decisions I made held weight and my movement had purpose. But the feeling that hadn't left my chest since that night was one I wanted to last a bit longer.

We hadn't gone more than a few hours without talking since then. Between the texts, FaceTime calls, and random voice notes in the middle of the night, everything was playing out the way it should have from the start. She'd even spent the night at the crib without my encouragement, just a random text in the middle of the night asking if I was available for cuddling. I didn't respond, just showed up a short time later and told her to bring her sexy ass downstairs.

That night, she fucked me so good, I was sucking her toes by the morning. It was something about new pussy that would have a nigga's head gone, but new pussy from a woman you cared deeply about made you think about the future. And seeing that I'd already envisioned what Danae would look like walking down the aisle, I was already ahead of the game.

As of today, Amil hadn't said anything to either of us about the cameras at the diner. That shit had Danae walking around on eggshells. I, on the other hand, was prepared to hear my sister's mouth if she did come across the footage. Part of me felt like if she had seen it, she was waiting for the opportunity to play it as her ace in the hole to get something out of me. The Libra in her wouldn't be able to help it.

"You overworking your brain again?" Grandma Lettie asked from where she sat across from me.

We were in her living room watching the latest episodes of *Love After Lockdown*.

"I'm a thinker, G."

"That's true, but when you get to thinking real hard, you get real quiet."

I sat up straight. "What are you, the grandchild whisper? How you just be knowing shit?"

"It comes with age, baby." She smiled. "How's Danae?"

"She's good. Out shopping for Key's Valentine's Day party and Mil's Galentine's Day dinner she's having later."

"Okay. A sponsored shopping trip, I hope."

I smirked. "You know it."

"You come from good stock."

Laughing, I nodded in agreement. "She's been opening up more. Letting me in little by little. She even spent the night."

G paused and looked at me over her glasses.

"Before you even start, she came on her own."

"Hey," she said with her hands up. "You just never know witchu, grandson. I know you ain't above a little kidnapping in the name of love."

We both laughed, and I waved her off. "Mannnn, it ain't never that serious."

She cut her eye at me, lips twisted like she didn't believe what I was saying.

"Aight. Aight. I might," I admitted.

She shook her head, still laughing. "And Grandma still love you, baby. And I'm happy for you too. For a minute there, I thought I was gonna have to pull up on Danae myself. You been driving us crazy."

I chuckled. "Damn. That bad?"

"Boy, yes. I was on the phone wit' ya daddy yesterday, telling him about it. He was cracking up. That's cause he knows he was just as bad when it came to ya mama."

I sighed, feeling the residue of grief that still held a piece of my heart come up. "I told Danae about my moms and what her suicide did to him."

"Did you tell her what it did to you? I think that's far more important considering she'll be with you and not your father."

"She asked me why I never gave the women I dated in my life my heart. I said I saw how it broke him after she died. And I didn't want that for me."

G pushed herself up off her favorite chair and slowly walked over to sit by me. "You can't build on a lie you've told yourself for years in order to maintain, Aura."

I squinted, and my forehead creased in confusion. "What I lie about?"

"The reason you never gave anyone you dated your heart wasn't because of what you seen your father go through. You never gave your heart because you couldn't give away something that was broken, baby."

"Ho..."

"I need you to hear this," she cut me off. "I watched your heart break in real time at thirteen-years-old when you sat in this living room, curled up in my favorite chair, questioning why God couldn't make your mother stronger. And what did I say to you then?"

I closed my eyes and felt her grab my hand the same as she did that day. "You told me it was okay to let my heart break and that the pain and the loss would lessen as time went on."

"And what else?"

"That my mom had to go to be free, but she'd send someone special to mend my broken heart when it was time. And when it was time, you knew I'd let you know."

I thought about Danae and felt goosebumps running up my arms once I opened my eyes.

"That's the woman you asked me to pray for," G said with a small smile. "This is why I didn't want you to rush it. Danae was the woman that your mother sent to fill that void in your heart. She can deal with both, Aura, the boss in the streets. But with a whole heart, you're able to give her Aura Sullivan, the man."

"Hey, they both men. Come on now, G." I laughed, wiping the corners of my eyes where tears had welled up.

"Boy, hush. You know exactly what I mean. Your mom would be proud." She pointed a finger at me. "Don't forget what I said though. Make sure your love feels like fresh air and not suffocation."

"Understood."

She kissed my forehead and got up from the couch.

My phone rang on the coffee table. It was Enzo calling. I answered without hesitation.

"What's good?"

"On my way to the Bronx," he said. **"Pulling up on KJ's uncle about that weed shit."**

"How far are you?" I put the phone on speaker to put my coat on.

"Like forty-five minutes."

"Bet. I'll meet you over there."

"Nigga always wanna get in on the action." He chuckled.

"Shiiiddd. Them niggas betta not even act like they want problems. I'll meet you halfway."

"It's Mitchells projects so meet me by the Western Beef."

"Aight." I ended the call and picked my keys up from the couch. "I'm out, G. I love you."

"Love you too!" she yelled out from wherever she'd disappeared to in the back of the house.

I headed out the door with one steady thought at the front of my mind. We were going to the Bronx to get an understanding about family. However, if we weren't received well, we could take the Sullivan approach. That approach usually involved guns and shit. Either route, I planned to leave the conversation with an understanding.

By the time I pulled into the parking lot at Western Beef, the sun had gone down. I spotted Enzo's car near the back and pulled up next to it, rolling my window down.

"Leave your car here and hop in mine," I told him.

"Why we gotta leave my shit? Why we can't leave yours?"

"Cause there's a $200,000 price difference between this Urus and that Q5."

"Nigga, this my work car," he said, hopping out of the driver's seat.

Enzo was dressed like he'd just left the office with a black Lacoste sweater, black slacks, peacoat, and a pair of black Pradas on his feet. I was dressed down in a Thom Browne sweatsuit, constructs, and a leather coat. We both looked and smelled like we made money, just in different areas.

"We some smooth looking niggas," I commented once he was in the passenger seat.

"All facts." He dapped me up, and I pushed forward.

Pulling up to the first building on the corner of Alexander Avenue, we double parked. I'd never done business with Koric or his brother directly because I didn't deal on that level. I paid people to be in certain places and handle certain deals so that I could focus on the big shit. However, I knew his face after looking into him when Thyri was first introduced to Enzo. His brother, Kaleb, Thyri's ex-husband, had removed himself from this part of the game and took his talents down to Georgia to lock down the fraud market. I assumed Koric's heart remained in New York because he stayed in the Big Apple after having already made a name for himself in the Bronx.

The front of the building was busy with activity as the block boys settled into their usual formations, one group making sales and the other serving as lookouts. No real security. I couldn't say that I expected much. Enzo and I stepped out at the same time and walked up to the entrance, ignoring the stares along the way. My father taught me early on that it wasn't how you pulled up when you had a whole crew with you that let niggas know what time it was. It was the kind of statement your presence made when you were small in numbers that showed power. And by the way heads turned when we moved, I knew he was right.

As we approached the lobby door, a guy stepped out from the group. "What's good? Who y'all here to see?" he asked like he was the spokesperson for the building.

I hated to be questioned, but I had an understanding that we were unfamiliar faces in their hood, so the alert was warranted.

"We here to see Koric," Enzo replied evenly. "He around?"

The nigga looked us up and down like he could somehow measure the reason for our visit by what we had on.

"Who y'all?"

I heard Enzo sigh before he pulled his gun and pointed it at dude's head. "Look, 50 Cent. If ya name ain't Koric, then miss me wit' the twenty-one questions, my nigga."

Ol' boy's facial expression went from hard to sheer fear in a matter of seconds. I didn't bother reaching for my gun. Instead, my eyes scanned the group, checking for any movements. Everybody looked either confused or shocked. It was clear that they didn't know whether to reach for a gun, if they had one, and risk their peoples' brains painting the lobby door or take their chances. *Their hesitance will be their downfall somewhere down the line,* I thought.

Before anyone could decide what to do, a tall, brown skinned nigga who resembled KJ walked out with a Glock pointed in our direction. "Fuck is going on out here?" he snapped.

I couldn't take a nigga serious in a hoodie, pajama pants, and a pair of constructs. Clearly, someone had alerted him, and he came downstairs in what he had on. I shook my head and ran my hand over my waves.

"Koric?"

"Who's asking?"

"Y'all niggas 'bout to blow me wit' that shit," Enzo said. Next to Pryce, his patience was thin as hell. "We asking. And I don't even know why. You look just like KJ."

His lip curled up in a frown. "How you know my nephew?"

"That's what we came here to chop it up about. We gon' do that with or without guns? Either way is fine with me," I said, talking to Koric but still keeping my eye on the crowd at the same time. I had to see everything moving.

"Take the burner from my mans' head first."

Out the corner of my eye, I could see Enzo drop his arm and hold his gun at his side. Koric did the same.

"Let's go to the street before I pop one of these lil' niggas," Enzo suggested.

"We can talk right on the sidewalk." Koric put his hand out as if to tell us to walk ahead of him.

"Fuck we look like, one of ya hoes? We ain't walking ahead of you. And bring this nigga if you don't feel safe." He pointed at the guy who still looked shook up from the gun being put to his head.

We all managed to get to the sidewalk without incident, and Koric told his mans to step back a few feet to give us privacy.

"So, wassup?"

"Well, first, I'm Aura, and this is my cousin, Enzo."

"Yeah, and?"

"You hostile than a bitch, ain't you?"

"Man, y'all niggas pulled up in my hood and put a gun to my mans' head then mention my nephew. Yes, I'm hostile, as any other nigga in my position would be. The fuck."

He had a point, so I didn't argue.

"Look, nigga, we're here about our nephew, Cortez," Enzo cut in. "He's best friends with KJ. Recently, they got into some trouble at school for selling weed that you gave them. We're here simply to get an understanding. Under no circumstances are you to give that shit to our nephew. I really don't even understand why you gave it to KJ, but I don't wanna overstep, so I'm just gonna speak on the strength of mine."

Koric's posture stiffened. "First off, nigga, I don't like yo' tone. Second, I didn't give your nephew shit. And as far as KJ, that's family, so that's none of y'all concern."

"You know what? I changed my mind. I am gonna overstep." Enzo stepped forward so that he was in Koric's face. "Don't give that shit to my nephew or your nephew. They good kids, and we can't teach them to be good men by giving them weed to sell or use. And if you don't know who I am, let me make it clear. Enzo Sullivan. Thyri is my woman, so KJ is my family. You can take heed to this courtesy call, or we can handle any discrepancies right here."

"You niggas done with this whole speech? Cause I got shit to do," Koric finally let out after a pause.

"So long as we're clear," Enzo replied, taking a step back.

"Yeah, aight." Koric went to turn away, and I called out to him. He stopped but didn't face me.

"Aye, Koric, you got a good thing going here as far as your hustle goes. Remember, the train keeps moving as long as the conductor is in place, bruh."

He looked over his shoulder and frowned slightly.

"I'm the conductor," I continued. "And I'd hate to have to let you off before you reach your destination. It's best that we're all on one accord."

I let him know, in not so many words, that I was the HNIC and would cut off his supply if need be. He didn't reply, but I hoped he understood.

CHAPTER 14

The Title

ENZO

We hopped back in Aura's car, and I could see Koric walking up the steps slowly, stopping at the top and staring at the car as we drove away. They were all staring. And as the projects faded, becoming small the farther we drove away, the more my jaw tightened.

"That nigga could be a problem," I said to Aura.

"One that I don't mind fixing if need be."

I sat back in the seat, replaying the conversation. "Yeah. Need to keep an eye on him in the meantime. I sense treachery."

Aura didn't hesitate. "I'm already on it. If he get to moving off, I have no problem turning the projects dark and cutting off his supply."

I knew it wasn't a threat but simple cause and effect.

As we pulled back into the Western Beef parking lot, my phone chimed in my pocket. Taking it out, there was a text notification from Thyri. The tension in my chest shifted into something calm.

> Thyri: Hey, I know you're probably busy. I was just reaching out to see how KJ did today and how your day's going.

Me: Wassup, beautiful? My day was interesting. I got a good report back from the ladies on KJ. They said he handled every task they gave him, and he flirted his way through each one of them. LOL

Thyri: Oh, my God. He's a mess. Care to share what was interesting about your day?

Me: Not right now. But we can talk about it in person. You still out shopping?

Thryi: Yep. Danae is dragging me to every store in Manhattan. She's really leaving no stone unturned.

Me: LOL. I bet.

Thyri: Oh, I meant to ask earlier. What size pajamas do you wear?

I frowned at the question, confusion setting in.

Aura glanced over at me. "What?"

"Nothing. I'm tryna figure out why Thyri just asked me what size pajamas I wear."

Thyri: Asking so I can pick up our matching pajamas for Kyiris' party.

"Never mind," I said to Aura. "I forgot about the theme for Key party."

"Oh, yeah." Aura nodded. "The come in ya drawls party."

I chuckled and responded back.

Me: Large top and large bottom. Don't pick me up nothing wit' no hearts and shit on it, Thyri.

She replied back immediately.

I stared at the screen for a few seconds, then it hit me. I hadn't even officially asked her to be my Valentine yet. I was out of pocket and had to get on that before the party this weekend.

"Yo, you asked Danae to be your Valentine yet?"

Aura looked up from his phone with his brow raised. "What you mean ask her? That's already understood. What other nigga gon' be her Valentine?"

I laughed. "Nigga, no, it ain't."

He blinked at me, face all screwed up like I had said something wrong. "We together. How it ain't understood that she my Valentine?"

"Women wanna be asked, bruh. Whether you're dating, engaged, or married, they wanna be asked at all levels."

"You asked Thyri yet?"

"Nah. That's why I brought it up cause I have to. We late as hell."

"So, let me get this straight. I'm supposed to formally ask something she should already know?"

"Yep."

"You know what? Fuck it. If that's the unspoken rule, then that's the rule. I ain't 'bout to have my baby feeling left out anyway, so Valentine's Day proposal it is. So, what you doing?"

I leaned back in the seat, thinking.

"We don't do simple, but we do thoughtful. It's last minute, so we might not be able to get no big shit done."

"Says who?" Aura countered. "It takes money to do big shit. We got money, so we can do big shit."

"Yeah, but the thought we put into it gon' mean more than the money we spent, feel me?"

He nodded. "True. I ain't tryna do nothing corny though."

"Define corny."

"Teddy bears holding stuffed hearts. It's overdone, and it ain't original. This our first Valentine's Day proposal. We gotta make it memorable."

"It ain't my first one. I asked Kennedy wack ass when we were together."

"And what you asked her with?"

I smirked. "A teddy bear holding a stuffed heart."

"Exactly." We burst out laughing. "Thyri deserves better."

"Facts."

The car went silent again, us both in our heads, trying to figure out the best way to make the new women in our lives feel special.

"I got it," he let out. "The Galentine's dinner at Mil's tonight. They both gon' be there."

I sat up straighter and smirked slightly. "We gon' crash it?"

"That sound aggressive as fuck." He laughed.

"But effective and intentional. And it'll be us officially letting everybody know wassup." I thought about the fact that Thyri and I hadn't officially announced that we were together and how I'd use the moment to do it.

"Bet. We gotta have something in hand when we pull up. I heard all that, *it's not about the money; it's about the thought,* shit you spittin', but I gotta ice my baby out."

"Oh, I'm on that. I'm just saying don't go rushing around throwing shit together. Gotta think it through." I looked at the time on his dashboard, and it read 5:45 p.m. "What time the dinner start again?"

"I think 8:30."

"Well, let's do the damn thing cause time is not on our side." I dapped him up and got out of the car to hop into mine.

I started it up and headed over to my mom's house where EJ was. She'd taken him out earlier on a movie date. She hadn't called or texted me the whole time, so I assumed it went well.

My mind drifted to Thyri as I drove. I thought about how she'd feel about me stepping to Koric and also revealing that we were together. I didn't know if she'd told her ex-husband yet. I really didn't know much about the relationship other than she was happily divorced, and he was involved in KJ's life. I felt like that was all I needed to know. So long as his being a present co-parent didn't affect us, I wasn't tripping.

I was pulling into my mother's neighborhood when my phone chimed. It was another text from Thyri. Unlocking the phone, there was a video loading. Once it loaded, I hit the play button. It was Thyri showing me a pair of black silk pajamas with a heart on the shirt pocket. The camera then panned to her face.

"So, I know you said you don't want all the hearts, but what about one heart? I think that's a good compromise. What you think?"

The video went off, and I called her. She answered on the first ring.

"**Hey, love.**" Her voice came through melodic.

"**Wassup, Ma? I was just calling to tell you that the pajamas are a yes.**"

"**Oh, good cause I already bought them.**" She snickered.

"**Mannn.**" I laughed.

"**What? I had to make you think you were involved. That's what we do in a relationship.**"

"**Con your man?**"

"**I like to call it making a decision that's best for the both of us.**" I could hear the smile in her tone.

"**Aight.**

"**You finished shopping?**" I asked, getting out of my car and opening the gate to my mother's townhome.

"**One more store then I'm headed home to get dressed for the night.**"

"**Okay, cool. Send me pictures.**"

"**Will do. Danae is driving tonight. You mind picking me up after and ummm... having your way with me?**" She flirted.

I smiled. "**I can do that.**"

"**Perfect. Talk later.**"

"**Aight. Be safe. Watch your surroundings.**"

"**Will do.**"

We ended the call, and I navigated my text thread and sent a message to Kyiris.

Me: Yo, Key. I need a favor.

Kyiris: Big favor or small favor?

Typing in the code to the door, I walked inside.

Me: You gotta determine that.

Kyiris: Aight, what you want?

Me: I need you to reach out to your homegirl at the flower shop and order me fifty long stem roses with the custom Will You Be My Valentine message on it.

Kyiris: Oh, that's doable. I got you.

I'd gotten her to buy in on the small favor first before I got to the big one.

Me: I need it tonight tho. And I need it dropped off to Amil's crib.

Kyiris: Now, wait a minute, nigga. You should've lead with all that.

I laughed out loud, knowing she was gon' have some smart shit to say.

Me: You can send it in an Uber Black. I'll pay. All I need you to do is make the call.

Kyiris: Smh. Alright wit' ya late ass.

Me: Preciate you. Love you.

Kyiris: Mmhmm. Love you too.

In this short time, I'd learned that Thyri loved simple things like morning texts, good night texts, random videos that I thought were funny sent to her on IG, and Edible Arrangements. She was easy to please, which made me want to make this Valentine's Day proposal special for her without all the theatrics.

"Daddyyyy." EJ came running at me full speed.

Thankfully, he had on grip socks because his head was no match for my mother's hardwood floors.

"I thought you'd be back late," she said, kissing my cheek.

"Nah. How was the movie?"

"It was good. He stayed quiet the whole time. You had to see him with a big bucket of popcorn and the slushy he tried to balance in his lap at the same time."

"That's Daddy big man." I picked EJ up and swung him over my back.

"So, what you got planned for Thyri for Valentine's Day? You need me to watch him?" We walked into the living room and sat down.

"If you could for a few hours, I'd appreciate it. Kyiris is throwing this "Will You Be My Boo" Valentine's Day party for the couples."

She chuckled. "One thing about my niece, she love a theme."

"And will drive everyone crazy about it. Ma, she created a whole group chat and been sending scheduled updates."

"She is my brother's child for sure. Oh, there's something I wanna show you. I'll be right back."

"Okay."

"Daddy." EJ called to me while climbing on my neck.

"Wassup, son?"

"Daddy, I play," he said, flipping off my neck onto the couch.

"I see. You better be careful fore Grandma get you for flipping on her couch."

"Get down, boy," my mother let out, catching him mid flip. "You ain't about to flip me into the emergency room." Sitting back down next to me, she handed me a piece of construction paper that EJ had colored on.

"What's this? A deconstructed family?" I laughed, holding it up to try to distinguish where the head began and feet ended. I did make out three circles and what I assumed was hair on two of them.

"Come here, EJ. Come tell Daddy what you drew," she prompted.

EJ crawled into my lap, and I gave him the paper.

"Who did you tell Grandma this is?" She pointed to the circle in the middle.

"EJ!" he shouted, pointing to himself.

"And who's this?" She pointed to the circle to the left of him.

"Daddy!" He grabbed my face and kissed my cheek.

"Mannn, get outta here." I playfully mushed him, and he put his small hands up like he wanted to fight. "Type shit," I muttered proudly.

"EJ, look." My mother called for his attention, pointing to the circle on the right. "Who's this?"

"That's Mommy!"

My head snapped back slightly. My mother didn't laugh. She just glanced at me then back at the paper.

"What's Mommy name?"

"Tyri!" he shouted confidently.

I stared at the picture, wondering when EJ had started to put Thyri and mommy together in his little head. He traced the picture absentminded, not knowing he'd dropped a bomb bigger than anything Funk Flex could have done on the radio. I looked over at my mother, and she nodded once knowingly.

"That means something, Enzo," she said softly. "It means a lot. Children don't attach titles to people easily. But they do know who and what makes them comfortable and safe. I knew Thyri did that for my grandson by the way he latched onto her at the Christmas party. Her singing him to sleep that night when y'all were on the way to dinner further proved it."

I thought about what she said and agreed. I hadn't coached

him. And Thyri hadn't done anything other than show up as her authentic self. She didn't overstep. She didn't play the role of mommy to EJ. They just bonded, making it easy for him to get attached to her. Making it easy for me to know that she was the one. She adored my son and made him happy. In turn, that made me want to make her happy.

"When's the last time you heard from Kennedy?" she asked a question I never thought I'd hear from her.

"The night me and Thyri were out to dinner. She came by the table and introduced herself as EJ's mom then proceeded to tell me how we needed to be adults for his sake and let her see him."

"She did that in front of Thyri?"

"Yeah."

"And what did Thyri say? Because this gon' determine whether or not she can hang with the Sullivans. You know we'll cuss a bitch smooth out from here to LA with style and grace."

Smirking, I nodded. "Then, you'll be proud to know that she told Kennedy and her husband to get the fuck on but in a classy way due to the setting."

"My girl. And Ms. Kennedy has a husband, huh?"

EJ climbed out of my lap and handed me the remote off the coffee table. I turned on the TV for him and sat him up on the couch.

"A husband and a kid."

"I could say I'm surprised, but I'm not. That girl is trifling. Did her husband say anything to you?"

"Tried to but you know he ain't get far. I think he got the hint that I'm not the nigga you can just say shit to." I left out the part where I let him know that by breaking into their home and making it clear.

"It may be time to have your lawyer draw up them custody papers, son."

I shook my head. "I'm not tryna go to the courts and risk them giving her joint custody. Kennedy got her shit together, a husband, house, and she fits the look of a good mother, even though she's a deadbeat. And in the eyes of the court, I'm nothing but a single father with a business and plenty money coming in, who's been taking care of his son for the last two years. They don't care about how she walked away. All they gon' see is she's here now."

"I hear where you're coming from. But..."

"There's no buts, Ma. I'm not doing it."

"And if she decides to beat you to it?"

"She won't be around long enough to have the first visit." I checked my watch and saw that it was getting late. I had to catch the Edible Arrangements store before it closed. "I'ma take him home tonight. EJ, go get your shoes." Folding the picture up, I put it in my pocket.

He slid down off the couch and ran to the back.

"I love you, son." She patted my back.

"I love you too, Ma."

After putting on EJ's shoes and coat, we headed outside. The air was cooler than it had been when I arrived. I strapped EJ into his car seat, shut the door, and paused for a second before walking around to the driver's side.

My son had given Thyri a title that she'd obviously been living up to in this short time. I had a choice to make. I could treat it like it was something casual or move like it was becoming permanent. Seeing as anything I put my time and energy into always worked out in the end, I was choosing the latter.

CHAPTER 15

Galentine's Day Surprise

THYRI

Danae and I stood in line at Auntie Anne's pretzel stand like we didn't already know the menu by heart. I was currently having an internal debate on whether I should go salted or have cinnamon sugar on my pretzel. We'd been walking around the mall, in and out of stores non-stop, and my stomach was touching my back. While Danae stood tall beside me like she hadn't been powerwalking the whole time, my feet were politely asking for downtime.

"Next in line," the girl behind the counter called to us.

Danae ordered first. "I'll take two originals. What you getting, Thyri? I'll cover it."

"I'll have two cinnamon sugars with extra icing."

"Ooop, not you tryna splurge on my dime," she said. "Charge the extra icing separately please." Danae went in her wallet to pull out cash.

"I'm sorry," the girl stated, confused.

Danae laughed. "I'm just joking, boo. Ring it all up."

She paid, and we were handed our pretzels. I slipped a five-dollar bill into the tip jar before we walked off to the food court to sit down. The smell of butter and sugar wafted up my nose as I tore through the packaging. I was all too happy to devour the pretzel, no drink needed.

"Okay," Danae said, biting into her pretzel. "We came in here to get an outfit for tonight and matching pajamas for Saturday night. Explain to me again how we ended up with all this?"

She pointed to the bags that sat on the side of us.

"I don't know," I replied, chewing. "I didn't go nearly as hard as you."

She counted my bags out loud and shook her head. "Survey says, you a baldhead lie. I have six bags; you have five."

"Exactly. One bag more than me." I smirked and chewed, watching people walk past with their bags full of impulse buys just like us.

"What's up with KJ?" she asked.

"He had his first cleaning assignment today. Enzo said he did good. Listened and didn't give anybody a hard time."

She nodded approvingly. "That's right. Work his ass. I still can't believe he was up at them people school selling the devil's lettuce."

I laughed so hard, I choked on my pretzel. "The devil's lettuce, Nae?" I repeated.

"Yeah. That's what it is."

"You sound like an old lady when you say it though."

She shrugged, finishing her first pretzel and checking the time on her phone. "We need to start heading to the car. It's getting late, and I wanna be on time to the dinner."

"Okay." I wrapped up what was left of my pretzel and picked up my bags.

We started walking toward the parking garage, both of our stomachs settled now that we'd put something in them.

"Any update on when Poppa D should be coming home?"

"They said it's looking like next month."

"Okay. They 'bout to free the GOAT finally. It's been time."

"I know, right? But girl, quiet as it's kept, I don't think he tryna come home with me. I think he's making plans to move in with his boo."

"Aunty Fawn?"

"Mmhmm."

"Ooouuu." She snickered. "Yo' daddy just too cool fa me."

"For me too."

We made it to the car, and she popped the trunk. Placing our bags neatly inside, I stepped back and shook my head.

"Can you believe I was just in there shopping for a man? Like girl, I got a man after a whole year of swearing them off."

She laughed. "No. Can you believe I was just in there shopping for Aura? My man, Aura." Hitting the unlock button on her car, she walked over to the driver's side and got in, while I made my way to the passenger side. "Not only did I buy the pajamas for Aura, but I bought him a two-hundred-and-fifty-dollar bottle of cologne. Just swiped my card like it was some shit I did on the daily. The di..." She stopped herself and looked straight ahead, starting up the car.

Leaning over, I tapped her shoulder. "Ummm, the what? I didn't catch that last part, boo."

"Nothing," she said quickly, keeping her eyes on the steering wheel.

"Oh, hell naw. You definitely was about to share something, and the class is listening, babes."

She laughed sneakily. "Well, the class needs to move onto another subject."

"Nae, we don't do that. You started the sentence. Go head and finish." I sat up in my seat, refusing to snap my seatbelt until she told me something.

"I was about to say... my last dinner shift at the diner put some things into perspective."

"You know what? Since you being all hush bout yo' business, yet somehow always wanna know mine, I'ma let you make it. But you got 'til this weekend to dish, heffa, or I'm never giving you my tea again."

"Now, that's a lie. You know you love to fill my cup. But I'm gon' tell you about what went down wit' me and my man soon. You just better be ready to listen and not judge." She blew me a kiss and pulled out of the parking spot.

We'd decided to get dressed together at my place in order to save time. I was glad she suggested it because now I had a reason for Enzo to pick me up. I just wanted to cuddle up under him, while he rubbed my back and kissed my face. The man was amazing and kept finding ways to confirm that I'd made the right choice by giving him a chance. Him helping me out with KJ's punishment put him in a new light as well.

I told my father about it, and he was all for the way I was disciplining KJ. He also mentioned that Enzo was taking the right approach in the way he had my back. He didn't overstep, and KJ seemed to be okay with it. To me, it showed that he wasn't trying to force his way into KJ's life. Instead, he was going with the flow.

By the time we made it to my house, it was seven o'clock. The dinner started at 8:30, giving us little to no time to prep and get ready. I looked over at Danae once we grabbed our bags and walked onto the sidewalk.

"I know. We need to hurry up," she said. "I just gotta jump in the shower, and it won't take me no time to get dressed."

"Same."

I unlocked my door, and the smell of Pine Sol hit me immediately. That wasn't normal unless I was doing the cleaning. Pushing the door open, we stepped inside to find KJ in the kitchen mopping. My brows lifted because KJ didn't mop. The most he'd do was Swiffer some shit and leave the dirty pad stuck to the bottom. He glanced up once he heard us.

"Hey," he said flatly.

"Wassup?" I replied with a hint of skepticism.

Danae stepped from behind me, taking in the scene. "Not Bob Marley actin' like he don't wanna speak."

KJ's lips twitched, and I heard a chuckle despite him trying to remain stone faced.

"Hey, God Ma," he spoke.

"Oh, okay. Cause I was about to get on yo' head. You know you speak to ya favorite when I come through." She walked over to him, and he gave her a hug.

"How was your day?" I asked, setting my bags down and embracing him the same way.

"It was cool. Busy."

"Good," Danae cut in. "The busier you are, the less you wanna get high. You should change the furniture around next. Get some Feng Shui going on up in here."

"Girl, please." I couldn't help but to laugh because she always did the most.

"Alright. Lemme go take my shower. You need to get a move on too, Butterfly." Picking up her bags, she headed to the back of the house.

"I'm going out tonight. I'll be back in the morning. You have an idea of what you wanna eat for dinner?"

"Not right now."

"Okay. When you get hungry, just order something off Door Dash. Text me if you need me."

"Alright."

"Make sure you empty that mop bucket and clean it out when you're done."

I left him standing in the kitchen and went back to my room to transform. I was excited about tonight. And if I was honest, I was more excited about ending it with Enzo. But I loved me a good girls' night. If I knew nothing else, I knew the Sullivans could put on a shindig.

We showed up to Amil's condo late with apologies on the tips of our tongues, ready to drop them as soon as we saw her.

"Just ghetto," Danae uttered, checking herself out in the elevator mirror.

"Girl, shut up. We ain't late on purpose," I said, fixing my bodysuit so that it didn't have that annoying space at the coochie part.

I'd chosen to wear a red, long-sleeved bodysuit that had the thumb cut out at the sleeves and a pair of black Azalea Wang thigh high boots. With the outfit being simple, I made sure to make it pop with my jewelry and a cropped fur coat. Danae had on a pair of black jeans that held her thighs hostage and made her already big booty look plumper than usual. She did a leather bustier with a fur and red thigh high boots. Our hair was freshly done, and makeup was intact, giving bitches the blues for sure.

We could hear the music as soon as the doors opened on Amil's floor. Rihanna's *Say It* played loudly, and we danced our way to the door. We were Rihanna stans. With the music being loud, Danae decided to call her and let her know we were outside. She came to the door a few minutes later.

"Heyyyy, boo." She greeted Danae with a hug and did the same with me.

I took in Amil's attire and donned her the main character instantly. She was dressed in a silk red pajama set with her hair pinned up, making it clear that she was just the host and would not be partaking in any manual labor. I absolutely lived for her.

"Come in. Everybody just got here a few minutes ago. I'll take your coats."

That made me feel so much better about being late, but I still apologized. "Sorry we're late."

"Girl, don't even worry about it. I just walked out here, and this my house." She laughed.

When we stepped inside, it felt like a curated Galentine's for the IT girls, from the red lighting that cast over the entire front of her house to the setup in her entryway. A tall gold stand sat in the front with a sign that said, **"GET IN, CUTIE, IT'S GALEN-TINE'S DAY."**

Next to it was a table draped in red satin with glasses filled with strawberry lemon drops and some with champagne. Beside the drinks sat a guest book with a fur pen between the pages. One side of the page said, **"Leave Your Mark If You're A Sullivan"**, and the other said, **"With Love, From Dope Ass Friends"**.

Naturally, I went to sign the friends' side, and Amil stopped me.

"Girl, please. You betta leave your mark." She then turned to Danae. "And you betta not even think about signing that side."

Danae grinned, and I laughed, signing as a Sullivan, even though I wasn't one. I guess when the men took you in, so did the rest of the family. We stepped farther inside and turned the corner to see her whole living room decked in red and black. Red and black heart shaped balloons floated in the ceiling, and the pillows that aligned the huge sectional were also black and red. Real roses in vases were placed throughout the space, making for another level of cutesy.

"Hey, ladies." Amil spoke to everyone who had gathered in her dining room. "The last of our guests have arrived. Most of y'all know Nae and may remember her cousin, Thyri, from the Christmas party. I'm gonna formally introduce them as Aura and Enzo's women."

"Finally!" one of them yelled out, making me and Danae laugh.

I recognized a few Sullivan faces from the Christmas party, along with Kyiris and Marli. The ladies all gave genuine smiles and stood to hug us once we got to the table. There were ten women at the table, six of them cousins and four of them friends of Amil's. Everyone understood the color assignment and was dressed in either red or black or a mixture of both. The energy in the room felt warm as we took our seats across from each other and sipped on our lemon drops.

"Drink and get comfortable, ladies," Amil instructed. "Dinner will be out in a minute."

We all fell into conversation like we'd known each other for years – conversations of what we did for a living, our kids, who did our hair and nails, and the latest celebrity gossip amongst a few other things. Danae and I usually stayed close together until we got a good feel of the people we were around, but the vibes in the room had us jumping from one conversation to the next, not missing a beat even when the food came.

"Okay, ladies," Kyiris stood after about an hour of eating and two rounds of drinks, asking for everyone's attention, same as she had the night of the Christmas party. "We're gonna head to the living room for games."

"I want y'all to know this was not my idea," Amil joked, standing from the head of the table with her champagne in hand.

"They know, and you're welcome." Kyiris stuck her tongue out and ushered everyone into the living room.

Everyone found a seat on the couch that I knew was comfortable before I even sat down.

"Okay. I figured the best game to play is Never Have I Ever," Kyiris suggested. "And y'all been drinking, so I know y'all 'bout to spill y'all tea." She laughed and sat in between Marli and Amil. "I'll start. Never have I ever faked a call to get out of a bad date."

One of Amil's friends, Justine, was the only one to drink.

"That's childish as hell, Jus." Amil giggled.

"Shiiiddd, no, it ain't. These niggas be crazy out here. I even started giving my real number when I'm approached in the street. They be wanting to call you right then and there. Be safe now, block later."

"I'm witchu on that," Marli agreed. "Only a nigga gon' have to feel a hot one pressuring me."

"Period." Their cousin, Shawna, cosigned.

Marli went next. "Never have I ever gone through a man's phone while he was sleep."

The whole room drank, and we all burst out laughing, not the least bit shamed.

"Bitch, I'll go through a nigga phone while he up," Justine said. "I don't fuck around."

We all went around the room with our Never Have I Ever statements, each response funnier than the last. It was light at first until we got to Danae, who decided to go last.

"Never have I ever ate a man's ass."

All eyes darted around the room to see who would drink, and when their cousin, Shameka, took a small sip, we howled, laughing.

Amil popped up from the couch. "Oh, my God! Meka, forreal? Bitch, gimme my wine glass." She jokingly reached for it, and Shameka doubled over in laughter, clutching her stomach.

"It was the nigga birthday. Goddamn."

"I wouldn't give a damn if it was Martin Luther King birthday," I said, shaking my head. "I draw the line."

"Well, why they put a gland in there that make you cum then? Don't knock it 'til you try it."

We all shook our heads, and she just shrugged, taking another sip of her champagne.

"Okay. My turn, my turn," Toni, another one of Amil's friends, stood to ask her question.

I didn't know why, but the way she stood made me feel like I wasn't going to like her question.

"Never have I ever... dated a killer."

The room went quiet for a few seconds, then a couple glasses tipped. Danae raised her glass slowly and took a sip but didn't look in my direction. That confused me a little, coupled with the look Toni was giving me.

"What?" I asked, wondering why she was staring me down.

"Oh, nothing, boo. I just figured since you're dating En..."

"If you don't move around wit' that messy ass shit, Toni," Kyiris cut in sharply, shooting her a deadly look that made her go quiet.

The tension heightened when I saw Amil give her the same look and shake her head slowly. I was even more confused then.

"Gimme a sec. I gotta step outside," Kyiris announced before standing. "Don't ask shit else, Toni."

The looks lingered once Kyiris left the room, and I still didn't know what the hell was going on that had the room so tense.

"So, yeah," Shawna spoke up, cutting the silence. "I made dessert. Come to the kitchen to taste, heffas."

Everyone got up from their seats, including Danae, but I pulled her back down.

"What the hell was that about?"

"Shit, beats me." She shrugged. "Let's go get dessert. Shawna bakes her ass off." She pulled me up from the couch, and I decided to let the awkward moment pass for now.

As we made our way over to the kitchen, Kyiris returned, and this time, she had Enzo, Aura, and EJ with her. Both Enzo and Aura had gifts, and she had EJ in her arms.

"I found two hobos and a baby out front. Do they belong to either of y'all?" She smiled, and Enzo mushed the back of her head. "Keep your hands to yourself, nigga." She swatted him.

"Oh, I most definitely know the baby," I said, walking over with my hands out for EJ. His head popped up when he heard my voice. He almost leaped out of Kyiris' arms to get to me.

"Tyriiii!" he exclaimed.

"Hi, my baby." I took him from her and kissed all under his neck, making him laugh, and everyone let out synchronized awws.

I could see Aura making his way over to Danae, who stood over to the side with a wide grin.

"Can I get some of that love?" Enzo asked once he was in front of me.

"Is that stuff mine?" I pointed to the roses wrapped in Dior paper and the Edible Arrangements bag.

"It is."

"Then this love is also yours. Put your neck up please."

He laughed and leaned in to kiss me. "Girl, please."

I kissed his lips a few times before EJ decided that was enough PDA.

"What y'all doing here?" Amil asked.

"We're here to ask these two beautiful ladies a question," Aura said, holding Danae by her waist and staring into her eyes like it was just the two of them in the room.

"Don't call my woman beautiful, my nigga," Enzo let out, making Aura laugh.

"No disrespect."

I smiled, lifting EJ up on my hip. "What is it you wanted to ask me?" I questioned, redirecting his attention.

"Will you be my Valentine?"

I answered without hesitation. "I sure will." I took the flowers from him and handed EJ over.

"This is too cute," Kyiris said.

We looked over at Aura to hear his Valentine's Day proposal.

"Will you be something to a nigga that you already know you are?" Aura asked Danae, who scowled at him.

"No," she responded and went to walk away, but she didn't get far once he pulled her back.

"I'm just playing, baby. Will you be my forever Valentine? You got me straight trippin', boo."

We all laughed, and Danae couldn't help but to join in, giving him a yes before wrapping her arms around his neck to kiss him.

"I tired, Daddy," EJ said.

I thought about using him as my excuse to leave. I mean, technically, Enzo was my ride home anyway.

"I hate to do you like this, but I'm taking my woman home wit' me," Enzo announced, and I was happy that I didn't have to be the bearer of bad news.

"I'ma let you have it this time," Amil said, walking over to kiss my cheek then EJ's. "Thank you for coming, boo. I enjoyed your company. I'll grab your coat."

"Thank you for having me."

I gathered my stuff, waved by to Danae and the rest of the ladies, then left with my Valentines, with an S, because if EJ was around, I made sure he was included.

EJ WAS KNOCKED OUT IN HIS CAR SEAT BEFORE WE GOT on the highway. I glanced back at him, smiling at the way his head hung to the side slightly.

"He must've played hard today."

"He did a little bit of everything. My mom took him to the movies earlier, then he ran around her house. When I picked him up and took him home, he ran amuck there after I fed him. I think he burnt out now."

"Oh, most definitely."

Enzo reached over and squeezed my thigh. "You fuckin' that red up."

"Thank you, baby. I had a really good time tonight. Amil did her thing."

"Yeah. When I walked inside and saw the sign, I knew she wasn't fucking around."

"You mean when y'all crashed the party?"

"For good reason." He winked.

The Never Have I Ever game came to mind out of nowhere. I thought about that killer question and decided to ask him about it. Before I could, my phone rang. The ringtone for Kash Dolls' *Baby Boy* played, and I knew it was KJ calling.

"Hey. Everything okay?" I answered.

"Yeah. Dad wanted me to call you on three way. Dad, you there?"

I instantly caught an attitude. Kaleb had been trying to call me the last couple days, and I had been purposely ignoring him because I didn't like the way our last conversation ended. It was a privilege to speak to me, especially when we had a teenage son who he could call whenever he wanted to. The fact that he was trying to use KJ to force me to talk to him was not cool. Plus, this wasn't a good time. I was riding with my man, and I didn't want him to see me all worked up behind Kaleb. Still, to show KJ that I could be an adult, I held the line.

"Yeah, I'm here." Kaleb's voice came through. **"Wassup, Thyri?"**

"Hey," I replied dryly.

"I ain't calling on no bullshit. I just wanted to apologize for how I reacted last time. You know, hanging up on you and shit."

"Oookay," I said, looking over at Enzo, whose eyes remained on the road, giving me as much privacy as he could, considering we were in close proximity.

"I spoke to KJ, and he says the dude you're seeing is cool and that he gave his blessing, so it's only right that I give mine too."

That was funny to me considering I wasn't looking for it.

"I spoke to my brother too. He said he got a visit from

your dude and his cousin. Apparently, they're Sullivans. Good people from what I hear. The type of people that I would entrust my kid with. You know, Koric ain't feeling niggas pulling up on his block, but I told him we'd do the same thing if the shoe was on the other foot, so he had to respect it. Plus, that nigga, Aura, holds the keys up there, and well... you know what that means."

"Mmhmm," I replied, ready to end the call.

"I ain't gon' tie ya line up too long though. Just wanted to call and say that."

"Okay. Thanks. Love you, KJ. I'll see you in the morning."

"Love you too, Ma."

I ended the call and held the phone up to my mouth.

"Everything aight?" Enzo asked.

"I guess so. That was KJ calling with his father on three-way." I told him the truth.

"Word? What he talkin' 'bout?"

"Called to apologize and give his blessing for us to date because KJ said you cool and he's good with it."

"I wasn't aware that you needed his blessing."

"I know. That shocked me too cause I never asked for it. But he also mentioned that you and Aura popped up on Koric."

He glanced over at me then focused back on the road. "We did. Had to get an understanding."

"I heard. Did y'all get into it?"

He snickered. "I don't get into it wit' people, Ma."

"Have you killed anyone, Enzo?" I came right out and asked.

"This week, no." He pulled into his driveway and turned off the ignition. Turning to me, he continued. "I own Sullivan & Co., but I'm also a contract killer. I've been doing it for years. I don't just go around killing people off impulse. I get hired to do a job, and I complete it. Do I like it? For the most part, yes. Now that you know that, you also need to know that no part of that world touches my personal life. I make sure of it."

"What happens to EJ if something happens to you?" I asked the first thing that came to mind.

"EJ has Sullivan blood running through his veins. He'll be straight for a lifetime. And now that we're together, that coverage extends to you and KJ."

"Okay," I said in a low tone, taking it all in.

"Do you have anything you wanna ask me?"

I shook my head.

"Can I show you something?"

"Yeah."

He reached into his pocket and handed me a folded paper. "Open it."

I did and smiled at the drawing. "A masterpiece." I giggled, giving EJ his props. "You gonna hang it up, or he drew this for me?"

"Nah. He drew it with you in mind."

I squinted, confused. "I'm not following."

"He said this is him. This is me. And this is Mommy. He said Mommy is you."

"Really?" I found myself getting choked up.

"My moms said children don't attach titles to people unless they mean something. Well, the same thing goes for me. I'm not asking you to be his mom or take on any roles you feel you can't handle. I'm just asking that you keep in mind what being with a man like me comes with now that you know the full scope of things."

I leaned over the center console and kissed his lips. "I can handle it."

He grabbed the back of my head and stuck his tongue in my mouth, kissing me nastily like there wasn't a toddler in the back-seat. Sucking my bottom lip into his mouth, he pulled back slowly.

"You're fired," he said simply. "Write down some things you wanna get into. Goals that you have or whatever. But after how nasty I'm 'bout to fuck you tonight, you can no longer be my nanny."

"En..."

"I got your severance package put together already. Come on, let's go inside."

I had never been happier to be fired in my life. I watched Enzo take EJ out of the car seat, and my heart swelled. I could see me building a family around the two of them, and one thing they'd never have to worry about was me leaving.

CHAPTER 16

Happily Ever After With A Sullivan

DANAE

If somebody would've told me that I'd be locked inside of Aura Sullivan's penthouse for two days and didn't feel the urge to run, I would've told them they were just as delusional as his ass. But here I was, laid across his couch, in his lap, with nothing on but a lace bra and his boxers. It was the most peaceful I'd been in a long time, and it felt so good. We hadn't left the house for anything since Amil's Galentine's Day dinner. Between fucking each other's brains out, debates over who had the best taste in movies, and Nerf gun wars that often ended with me hiding behind the kitchen island, yelling out I surrendered, we'd been in our own little world.

The amusement on my face when he ordered the Nerf guns off Instacart in the middle of one of our debates was pure comedy. This morning, we woke up, made breakfast naked, ate naked, and spent the rest of the day lounging around, watching movies, the movies we debated on. I smiled and squeezed my thighs together, thinking about how he'd come up behind me after breakfast while I loaded the dishwasher. Lifting my leg, he ate my pussy like he hadn't just had a hot meal.

His phone buzzed under me, pulling me out of my nasty thoughts. I sat up a little for him to grab it.

"Another reminder message from Kyiris," he said.

I laughed. "What she say?"

He held the phone up and read the message out loud.

"I'm 'bout to not go just to call her bluff."

I rolled over so that I was on my stomach and looked over at him. "Oh, you going. As a matter of fact, lemme show you the pajamas we wearing." I got up to grab the bag with our stuff in it from the side of the couch and pulled out the pajama set.

When I turned around to show him, I had to fight to keep a straight face. I held up the silk red set with pink hearts all around the top and bottom. It was loud, loud as hell.

"And who you think wearing that in or out the house witchu?"

I peeked through the sleeve. "This is our matching set, bae. Valentine's Day themed."

"You lost your mind if you think I'm putting that on. Shit, I wouldn't even let you walk outta here with that shit on. Go online and see what you can find on Macy's, Gap, something. But we ain't wearing that."

I couldn't hold it in any longer and burst out laughing. "You not about to have me out here looking crazy, baby?" I walked back over to him and straddled his lap.

"I said us, but clearly you don't give a damn about me."

"I do. The real pajamas are in the bag." Dipping my head, I kissed his lips.

"No pink hearts and bullshit?"

I kissed him again, talking into his lips. "No pink hearts and bullshit. Happy Valentine's Day, handsome."

He palmed my ass and kissed me back. "Happy Valentine's Day, baby. Lemme see the other pajamas cause yo' ass is too slick."

I giggled, getting up from his lap and grabbing the bag. "Here." I handed it to him.

"Aight. This is better." He nodded approvingly, taking the

deep red satin pajamas from the bag. "Burn that other shit." He pointed to the other set.

"The hearts are fire, bae."

"No. They belong in the fire. Go head and pack that shit up."

"I'll take 'em back to the store. In the meantime, we need to get up and ready. She said be on time."

"Aight. We'll shower together then, Ma. You ain't gotta beat around the bush about it."

"Oh, please."

He stood and picked me up over his shoulder. "Let's go, sexy."

I went to turn the shower on, and as soon as the steam filled the bathroom, I stripped.

"You puttin' this on?" He held out my shower cap that I wasn't ashamed to put on if it meant protecting my leave out.

"Thank you."

I stepped inside the hot water, and he got in behind me.

"How do you feel about tonight?" I asked him, while I washed his back.

"About what? The party?"

"That and us officially celebrating our first Valentine's Day together."

He turned around and wrapped his hands around my waist. "I look forward to any time I get to spend with you. I'm used to Key throwing parties, so I can't say I have a feeling about it. I'm looking forward to making this day special and memorable for us though."

"Me too."

He kissed my nose then proceeded to wash me from my head down to my feet. Once he was done, my body felt so relaxed, I wanted to lay down. We stepped out, and he wrapped a towel around me then around his waist.

"Before we go, we gotta do something."

"What's that?" I asked, sitting on the edge of the bed.

"Exchange gifts."

"Oh. Duh. Hold on." I grabbed the Macy's bag that had been sitting on his dresser and handed it to him.

He pulled out the Tom Ford Ombré Leather cologne and sniffed the box. "You bought this?"

"Yeah."

"What you know about men cologne? Some overly friendly nigga at the counter help you?" he questioned while opening the box.

"No. An overly friendly woman." I laughed.

He sprayed it once in the air and smelled it. "Yeah. This shit smell expensive. It got Aura Sullivan written all over it."

"I know. Now read the card."

I'd handwritten a note from my heart that I wanted him to read. I watched him open the card and read it silently before looking up at me.

"You serious about us, Danae?" he asked quietly.

"I am."

Nodding, he walked over to his nightstand and pulled out an envelope. Sitting down on the bed, he gestured with his head for me to come over. I did and sat on his lap.

"Happy Valentine's Day, baby."

"Open it?"

"Nah. Read through it with your X-ray vision." He laughed.

"Shut up." I elbowed him. Opening the envelope, I peeked inside and already knew it was a check. "Aura."

"Baby, take it out. Wait, that didn't sound right. Never take it out." He winked. "But go head and finish opening your gift."

I took the check out and gasped when I saw the 'in the amount of' number. Sixty thousand dollars paid to Danae Anderson from Sullivan Realty.

"What the hell, Aura?"

"I ain't gon' lie. This wasn't your original gift. Your necklace is in the closet. But this check was most important. I watched you get diligent yesterday and apply for two apartments for your Airbnb business, while we were chilling out there watching *A*

Long Kiss Goodnight. We'll get into you not paying attention to the movie at another time."

I giggled and rolled my eyes.

"But I watched you take another step in going for what's yours, and I want to put my money where my mouth is and invest in you. This is for you to do as you please to get started once you get them. Pay up a few months' rent on each unit, decorate, a start-up cushion. Whatever you wanna do, just see to it that it gets done."

Tears fell before I could stop them. "This is so thoughtful, Aura. Thank you so much."

"You're welcome, baby." I wrapped my arms around his neck and hugged him tightly.

"You gettin' fucked tonighhhttt," I sang in his ear, and he slapped my ass to let me know that he'd heard me.

WHEN WE WALKED INTO THE VENUE FOR KYIRIS' PARTY, I quickly concluded that everybody that was complaining about those reminders she sent needed to apologize immediately. The DJ was doing his thing, and the couples had overstood the assignment and brought out their best pajamas. Kyiris wasn't exaggerating when she expressed how much time and effort she'd put into getting things together. The heart shaped light installations that glowed along the walls as we came in was the most unique thing I'd ever seen. Farther inside was a heart shaped balloon arch that was too cute.

I pointed out the photo booth station with a custom sign that said, "Will You Be My Boo?" to Aura, letting him know that we'd be making a few stops there. Then, she topped it off with a full kissing cam set up near the DJ booth. And that was just the big things that I saw. If she went big on that stuff, I just knew she took her time with the little details.

"Bae, Kyiris really did her thing. You can't even front."

Aura scanned the room. "She don't never do nothing half ass. She definitely took it there with this."

We made it on time like she requested, and I was glad we did because she had the biggest smile on her face when she saw us.

"Awww, y'all did what I said. If I wasn't such a gangsta, I would cry." She hugged both of us and complimented our pajamas. "In theme. I like it."

"You should've saw that other shit she almost had me put on."

Kyiris snickered, and I rolled my eyes.

"Shut up." I spotted Thyri across the way at the buffet getting food. "I'll be back, baby. I'm gonna go say hi to my cousin. And Kyiris, girl, when it's time to plan my wedding, the job as wedding coordinator is yours, boo."

I walked over to Thyri, giving hugs to the faces I recognized as I passed through the crowd.

"Hey, boo." I gave her a side hug.

"Heyyy." She kissed my cheek. "How you let me beat you here?"

"I don't know. I just know I'm on time, and that's all that matters."

"According to Kyiris, yes, it is." We both laughed. "You're glowing, and I love to see it."

"And so are you. It's that sprinkle of Sullivan, girl. I'm realizing that now."

"I agree."

I grabbed a plate and added a few things to it before walking over to where Thyri had a seat. I didn't get to sit down before Aura came over and pulled me by my arm over to the kissing cam.

"Come here."

"Okay," I said, confused.

Guiding me in front of it where we were in the spotlight, he reached over the DJ booth and grabbed the microphone.

"Wait, Aura," I whispered. "What are you about to do?"

Raising his hand, he signaled for the DJ to cut the music down. The room quieted, and all eyes turned toward us. I smiled nervously, and then my eyes darted over in Thyri's direction. I saw her mouth for me to relax, and I took a deep breath in and exhaled. Then, I looked over at Aura. He didn't look nervous or unsure. In fact, he looked certain about whatever he was about to do.

"What's good, everybody?" he began calmly. "I know this is a little impromptu, but I can't go another day without asking this woman this question. Most of y'all know I waited a long time for her fine ass to just give a nigga a chance."

My heart started pounding, and my hands became sweaty.

"She ran. I chased. She ran some more. I chased some more. But not only did I chase, but I prayed. And I had G pray. Pray that she kept me in mind while she was running and would eventually run into me. She did that. And now, we here in matching pajamas and shit at a family gathering."

A few whistles came from the crowd followed by applause. My hands began to shake, and the tears were welling up. When he dropped to his knee and pulled out a Harry Winston box, my hand flew to my mouth, stifling a scream.

"Wait, wait." My words came out muffled.

"I done waited long enough." He smirked, and laughter rippled through the room. "You've been a Sullivan in my head for quite some time. Now, I wanna make it official. Danae Ariel Sullivan, will you marry me?"

The room felt like it was spinning, but we were all standing still. I didn't feel fear. I didn't feel doubt. I was sure, sure that I wanted to be Aura Sullivan's wife.

"Yes," I breathed.

As if it were planned, the DJ dropped *Keep Me In Mind* by Eric Bellinger. The room erupted as he slid the rock on my finger. Baby, I was going to be a Sullivan, which would only further confirm that bitches weren't fuckin' with me.

THE END

160

Also by Nai

A Hitman's Gift For Christmas

A YN'S Muse For The Summer

Wizdom: Forever Your Gangsta

A Secret Love Affair With The Plug

Wrapped Up In A Hitta's Love For Christmas

Yours For The Taking

Seizing A Gangsta's Heart For The Summer

Thug Me The Right Way

Thug Me The Right Way 2

Thug Me The Right Way 3

A Summer To Remember With My Hitta

Snatched Up By A Hitta

Wet Dreams On Lockdown: The Unit Manager

Santa Sent Me A Real One For Christmas

Bossin' Up On The Plug

Bossin' Up On The Plug 2

In The Trenches With My Hitta

In The Trenches With My Hitta 2

Stealing A Queenpin's Heart

Stealing A Queenpin's Heart 2

A Piece of A Hustler's Heart

A Piece of A Hustler's Heart 2

A Thug's Love Mended My Heart

A Thug's Love Mended My Heart 2

A Summer To Remember With My New York Bae

A Summer Fling In New York

His Hood Love Gave Me Life

His Hood Love Gave Me Life 2

My Thug, My Sanctuary

Thug Kisses For Christmas

For The Love Of My Savage

Charge It To The Game

Charge It To The Game 2

Charge It To The Game 3

Author's Note

Fine Shii, I really tried my absolute best to give y'all a thick book, but I had to realize that's really not my ministry. I believe y'all have come to love me enough to know that. And before I give y'all fluff, I'll respectfully bow out the game. That said, I hope you enjoyed the story and know that I appreciate each page read, shared, all dat. Until next time, Fine Shii. And I still DON'T WANNA ARGUE!!

SWIPE FOR THE NEXT SULLIVAN...

U.A.D PRESENTS
THE PRYCE OF
LOVING A BOSS
NAI

Did You Enjoy?

Did you enjoy the read?
Let us know how much by leaving us a
review on Amazon and Goodreads.

Other Books By
URBAN AINT DEAD

Tales 4rm Da Dale

The Hottest Summer Ever

Hittin' Licks For The Holidays: Atlanta

Wet Dreams On Lockdown: The Nurse

How To Publish A Book From Prison

How To Invest In The Stock Market From Prison

First Summer Out With My Prison Bae

By **Elijah R. Freeman**

Despite The Odds

Despite The Odds 2

By **Juhnell Morgan**

Hittaz

Hittaz 2

Hittaz 3

Hittaz 4

Hittaz 5

Hittaz 6

Coldhearted

Coldhearted 2

Coldhearted 3

By **Lou Garden Price, Sr.**

A Hitman's Gift For Christmas

A YN'S Muse For The Summer

Wizdom: Forever Your Gangsta

Charge It To The Game

Charge It To The Game 2

Charge It To The Game 3

A Summer To Remember With My Hitta

Snatched Up By A Hitta

Santa Sent Me A Real One For Christmas

Wet Dreams On Lockdown: The Unit Manager

Thug Me The Right Way 2

Thug Me The Right Way 3

Seizing A Gangsta's Heart For The Summer

Yours For The Taking

Wrapped Up In A Hitta's Love For Christmas

By **Nai**

A Set Up For Revenge

A Set Up For Revenge 2

Wet Dreams On Lockdown: The Librarian

By **Ashley Williams**

Trickin' On A Heaux For Christmas

Homie Hoppin' For The Holidays

Wet Dreams On Lockdown: The Female C.O

Letters Of His Love

By **Telia Teanna**

The State's Witness

The State's Witness 2

The State's Witness 3

This Time Won't You Save Me

This Time Won't You Save Me 2

His Summer Side Piece

A Holiday Heist

Healing The Heart Of A Detroit Gangsta

Summer Vows With A Detroit Gangsta

The Promissory

The Promissory 2

A Gangsta's Last Kiss

What Do The Lonely Do At Christmas

Colliding Into Your Love

By **Kyiris Ashley**

Stuck In The Trenches

Stuck In The Trenches 2

By **Huff Tha Great**

Melted The Heart Of A Menace

Wet Dreams On Lockdown: Lieutenant Grace

By **P. Wise**

Merry Trapmas

By **Mia Sky**

Thug Me The Right Way

By **DiamondATL & Nai**

Wet Dreams On Lockdown: The Counselor

By **Paris Iman**

Wet Dreams On Lockdown: The Male C.O

By **Tamyra Griffin**

Wet Dreams On Lockdown: The Captain

By **TN Jones**

Wet Dreams On Lockdown: The Warden

By **Shawnice**

Atlantastan

Atlantastan 2

Atlantastan 3

By **Chris Green**

IN The Streetz

IN The Streetz 2

IN The Streetz 3

IN The Streetz 4

IN The Streetz 5

IN The Streetz 6

Hittin' Licks For The Holidays: Charleston

By **Tron Hill**

Hittin' Licks For The Holidays: New York

Bandemic

Bandemic 2

By **Freshh Moneyy**

Coming Soon From
URBAN AINT DEAD

Drill
The Hottest Summer Ever 2
THE G-CODE
Tales 4rm Da Dale 2
How To Build Your Credit From Prison
By **Elijah R. Freeman**

Despite The Odds 3
By **Juhnell Morgan**

The Pryce Of Loving A Boss
A Felon's Promise
By **Nai**

Kenzo Steele
By Kyiris Ashley

To Die For
By **Tron Hill**

Bandemic 3
By Freshh Moneyy